CAN SKY PULL IT OFF?

"If I was getting up a fan club," Sky said, "I'd start with you three right here."

"Hi, baby." Jennifer smiled at him.

"So what's this big meeting about?" Sky asked, checking his watch. "I'm kind of pressed for time."

"Sky." Jennifer took a deep breath. "The word around the school is that if you don't do better in your classes you're going to be dropped from the team."

"The coach didn't tell me that," Sky said. "You running the team now?"

"Lighten up, Sky," Tasha said. "Jennifer's trying to give you the word. If you keep failing your tests you will be off the team, that's a school policy."

18 Pine St.

Sky Man

Written by
Stacie Johnson

Created by
WALTER DEAN MYERS

A Seth Godin Production

BANTAM BOOKS
NEW YORK • TORONTO • LONDON • SYDNEY • AUCKLAND

RL 5, age 10 and up

SKY MAN
A Bantam Book / March 1993

Special thanks to Susan Korman, who gave a lot to this book, and to Betsy Gould, Amy Berkower, Fran Lebowitz, Linda Lannon, Michael Cader, Sharyn Skeeter, Margery Mandell, José Arroyo, Julie Maner, Kate Grossman, Ellen Kenny, and Lucy Wood.

18 Pine St. is a trademark of Seth Godin Productions, Inc.

ISBN 0-553-29723-6

Published simultaneously in the United States and Canada

Bantam Books are published by Bantam Books, a division of Bantam Doubleday Dell Publishing Group, Inc. Its trademark, consisting of the words "Bantam Books" and the portrayal of a rooster, is Registered in U.S. Patent and Trademark Office and in other countries. Marca Registrada. Bantam Books, 666 Fifth Avenue, New York, New York 10103.

PRINTED IN THE UNITED STATES OF AMERICA

RAD 0 9 8 7 6 5 4 3 2 1

For Helene

18 Pine St.

There is a card shop at 8 Pine Street, and a shop that sells sewing supplies at 10 Pine that is only open in the afternoons and on Saturdays if it doesn't rain. For some reason that no one seems to know or care about, there is no 12, 14, or 16 Pine. The name of the pizzeria at 18 Pine Street was Antonio's before Mr. and Mrs. Harris took it over. Mr. Harris removed Antonio's sign and just put up a sign announcing the address. By the time he got around to thinking of a name for the place, everybody was calling it 18 Pine.

The Crew at 18 Pine St.

Sarah Gordon is the heart and soul of the group. Sarah's pretty, with a great smile and a warm, caring attitude that makes her a terrific friend. Sarah's the reason that everyone shows up at 18 Pine St.

Tasha Gordon, tall, sexy, and smart, is Sarah's cousin. Since her parents died four years ago, Tasha has moved from relative to relative. Now she's living with Sarah and her family—maybe for good.

Cindy Phillips is Sarah's best friend. Cindy is petite, with dark, radiant skin and a cute nose. She wears her black hair in braids. Cindy's been Sarah's neighbor and friend since she moved from Jamaica when she was three.

Kwame Brown's only a sophomore, but that doesn't stop him from being part of the crew. Kwame's got a flattop haircut and mischievous smile. As the smartest kid in the group, he's the one Jennifer turns to for help with her homework.

Jennifer Wilson is the poor little rich girl. Her parents are divorced, and all the charge cards and clothes in the world can't make up for it. Jennifer's tall and thin, with cocoa-colored skin and a body that's made for all those designer clothes she wears.

Billy Turner is a basketball star. His good looks, sharp clothes, and thin mustache make him a star with the women as well. He's already broken Sarah's heart—and now Tasha's got her eyes on him as well.

April Winter has been to ten schools in the last ten years—and she hopes she's at Murphy to stay. Her energy, blond hair, and offbeat personality make her a standout at school.

José Melendez seems to be everyone's friend. Quiet and unassuming, José is always happy to help out with a homework assignment or project.

And there's Dave Hunter, Brian Wu, and the rest of the gang. You'll meet them all in the halls of Murphy High and after school for a pizza at 18 Pine St.

PINE

One

"So let me get this straight, Sarah." Kwame Brown lifted a string of cheese from his pizza slice off of his chin and into his mouth. "You're going to college so that you can help to destroy the world?"

"What are you talking about, Kwame?" Sarah Gordon demanded. She took her books off the table at 18 Pine St., where she was hanging out with her friends, and put them on the floor. "I want to *help* the world—that's why I said I might study medicine in college."

"Right," he replied, "but the problem is, if you study medicine you'll become a great doctor."

"Kwame"—April Winter stood up—"I'm getting some food. This is going to be one of your long 'ain't going nowhere' stories, isn't it?"

Kwame gave her a superior look. "I will ignore the lesser mind that fills the air with noise," he said. "I was merely pointing out to you ladies that great doctors may save a lot of lives, but they also directly contribute to the overcrowding of the world."

Tasha Gordon, Sarah's cousin, was handing April a dollar for a soda. "Well, Kwame, what do you suggest as a solution? Maybe while Sarah goes to medical school I should learn how to be a hit person. You know, then I can decide who to save and who to get rid of."

"Is that called balancing the ecosystem?" Jennifer Wilson asked. "And how come April has to get the drinks when we have a mere man in our presence?"

April sat down, handed Tasha's dollar to Kwame, and dug her own money out of the pocket of her jeans.

"I have to leave," Kwame protested. "I'm supposed to call a guy this afternoon about a set of Civil War books he wants to sell."

"The Civil War can wait," Tasha said. "Get one diet cola, two slices of pizza—what are you getting, April?"

"A slice and some fries," April responded.

"How can you eat pizza and french fries at the same time?" Sarah asked.

Kwame stood. "You people want anything else?"

"And one soda for me," Jennifer said. "And don't take all day getting it, either."

2

you want them, just buy them," she said.

"I wish it was that easy." Kwame sighed as he gathered up his books.

"See you tomorrow," Sarah said.

"Yeah."

The four girls watched as Kwame headed for the door.

"Kwame definitely didn't write that note," Jennifer said. "No offense, Sarah, but he seemed more interested in the books than you."

Tasha shrugged. "Maybe he's just hiding his feelings."

Kwame was only a sophomore, but he had been Sarah's buddy for a long time. Sarah liked his sense of humor and his dedication as a friend. She once wondered if he had a crush on her, but that had changed soon after Tasha had come to live with the Gordons. Kwame had fallen fast for Sarah's cousin. Tasha seemed to enjoy teasing Kwame—one day she was flirting with him and the next she was putting him off.

Sarah shook her head. "Jennifer's right—if it was Kwame, he wouldn't have split for some Civil War books."

April grinned. "Maybe he can't stand to be around you. Maybe you're driving him crazy with desire."

Before Sarah could answer, she saw Dave Hunter walk through the door. She smiled at him as he came over to the table.

5

Dave had been Sarah's next-door neighbor and good friend for as long as she could remember. But one day last summer, Sarah's feelings for Dave had changed. Suddenly, and in a very intense way, she had found herself thinking about him as a boyfriend. Since then, they had dated a few times, but they had agreed to cool it for a while. It was as if too much was happening too fast. Sarah was confused about Dave—she knew how great she felt when they were together, but she wasn't sure she was ready for the intensity and commitment that a relationship with Dave would take.

There was a part of Sarah that hoped Dave was her secret admirer. But deep down, she knew he wasn't the one.

Lately, Sarah thought, Dave had seemed a little cool toward her. She wanted to talk with him and work things out—he was too great a friend to lose, and maybe there was something more there.

Dave put one foot on Kwame's vacated seat and leaned toward the girls. "Ladies"—he grinned— "you are looking at one of the members of the greatest basketball teams ever assembled at Murphy High."

Tasha looked up. "Really? I thought you guys were having an average season—win some, lose some."

"We were until today," Dave answered. "On this historic day, our destiny has been changed."

6

"What are you talking about?" Sarah asked.

"It's not what, it's who. At practice today, Coach Green introduced us to a transfer from out of state, a forward named Bill Hodges. His team won the state championship last year and he poured in thirty-four points in the finals, including three dunks. With him on our team, no one in the league can touch us. And with him in our gym, you can bet the college scouts will be in attendance almost every night. Which means I can look forward to getting letters from a lot more schools than just Providence."

"This guy's really that good?" Tasha asked.

Dave nodded. "The man can jump so high, his nickname is Sky. He's meeting me down here in a few minutes. If you don't want to take my word for it, Tasha, you can challenge him to a little one-on-one."

Tasha grinned. "Maybe I will."

"Murphy High could take the championship this year!" Jennifer said. "Imagine the gym absolutely packed for the playoffs, all of—"

The arrival of Bill Hodges cut her short. Dave stood up. "Hey, Sky, over here!"

Sky indeed, thought Sarah. Although Dave was well over six feet tall, the new player seemed to tower over him.

Dave grabbed an empty chair and brought it over to the table. "This is Bill Hodges," he said. "Bill just transferred into Madison."

"I heard you play ball," Jennifer said. "How tall are you, anyway?"

"Six-seven," was the answer. "And everybody calls me Sky."

"Where are you transferring from?" Tasha asked.

"Countee Cullen High, in Baltimore," Sky said.

Sarah watched Sky as Dave introduced everyone. The new player was good-looking, even if he wasn't as fine as Dave. He had broad shoulders and a powerful build. And his hands were the largest she had ever seen. For a second, she was tempted to sneak a glance under the table where his long legs were stretched out—his feet must be massive, too! But the thing that was most noticeable about Sky was his gold. He wore five gold chains, three heavy ones and two lighter ones. He also had a small gold earring.

"So you're going to play ball with Murphy?" Tasha asked.

"If I can make the team," Sky answered. But the smile on his face said he was already on Murphy High's team.

"We hang out a lot at 18 Pine," Dave said. "It's where you find the most hip people at Murphy High. You'll probably run into Cindy, Steve, José, and my man Kwame before the week's out."

"Sounds good to me," Sky said, looking down at his almost new sneakers. "I have to go to the store across town and get some new leaps. Coach Green said he might give me some time in the game

8

tonight."

Dave decided to go with Sky and the two left together, turning a lot of heads as they went.

"Did you check out the size of that boy's feet?" Sarah asked her friends.

"He's got to have big feet to balance all that gold he wears," Jennifer said. "So did anybody present have a slight jump in the rhythm of her heart for that fine young man with all the gold?"

Tasha shook her head. "Not me. But I would like to see him play ball."

Jennifer grinned. "I'll check his game out for you."

"Thanks, Jennifer," Sarah said. "That's so kind of you!"

"Anything for my closest friends," Jennifer said slyly. "Anything at all."

Two

When Sarah and Tasha arrived home on Friday afternoon, it was like walking into a dance club. Allison, Sarah's eleven-year-old sister, had the television turned on to MTV while the CD player blasted out a reggae beat. As soon as Allison saw the two older girls, she pulled a Murphy High basketball schedule from her jeans pocket.

"What time is tonight's game?" she demanded.

Sarah grinned at her sister. "Since when are you interested in Murphy High's basketball team?"

"My friend Pam told me about this guy named Sky at school today. I really want to see him play."

"Pam was talking about him? How does she know him?" Sarah asked.

"Everybody's talking about him," Allison said.

"He was mentioned in today's newspaper."

"Can we turn off just one source of noise in this house?" Mrs. Gordon said as she came into the room. "And does anybody want to go shopping for rugs with me after dinner?"

"We can't," Tasha replied. "There's a big basketball game tonight. This new guy we have on the team is supposed to be superstar material. We're going to check him out."

"You must mean Sky Hodges," Mrs. Gordon said. "He's supposed to be quite a sensation."

Sarah's jaw dropped. Her mother already knew about Sky, too!

Mrs. Gordon smiled when she saw Sarah's astonished expression. "Everyone's heard about Sky Hodges, my dear!"

That night the auditorium was crowded with more people than Sarah had ever seen at a Murphy basketball game. The Murphy High stands were filled not only with students but also with adults and younger kids. A lot of people had obviously read the article about Sky and wanted to see him play.

The game against St. Regis was supposed to be an easy win for Murphy, but that wasn't how things turned out. The center from the other school was six feet eight inches tall and very strong. By the end of the first half Murphy was trailing by seven points. They were double-teaming Dave, and Sky still hadn't played.

"They know a lot about our team," Tasha observed. "They're not about to let Dave go one-on-one."

"Why isn't Sky playing?" Allison asked.

"The coach must have decided to have Sky come to a few practices before putting him into a game," Tasha answered.

The second half started off badly, with St. Regis getting the first seven points. Sarah thought the St. Regis team seemed pumped up, as if they could feel a win coming.

The game wound down until five minutes were left to play. Dave and Billy Turner had brought the team back a bit, but they were still behind by four points. When Dave lost the ball on a back court violation, Coach Green called time out. Sarah realized that the coach couldn't wait until the next game. Sky was going to play.

St. Regis brought the ball down, moved it around on the outside until a man was open, and then tried a three-point shot.

The ball hit the back of the rim and bounced high into the air. Dave leaped up to get the rebound and fired it over to Sky. The new player grabbed it, held it high above his head, and waited until the St. Regis team had moved downcourt to set up their defense.

Sky sent a bounce pass to Billy and then loped up the court.

13

Sarah watched as Billy brought the ball up and threw it to Dave. Dave cut across the middle and hooked the ball toward the basket. The ball hit the rim, then the backboard, and suddenly there was Sky, his hand high above the rim, poised to slam it through the hoop.

As the ball dropped through the net, the crowd went wild. St. Regis quickly dribbled the ball downcourt. Billy intercepted a pass, looked around, then passed it toward the foul line, where Sky was waiting. With one hand Sky caught the ball in front of a startled St. Regis player. The St. Regis player braced himself for the contact, but instead Sky twisted away, leaping at a crazy angle to get around the St. Regis player and put the ball softly against the glass backboard.

At that moment, everybody knew the game was over for St. Regis. Sarah turned and gave Tasha a high five. Sky wasn't just good, he was fantastic!

After the game, everyone headed to the Gordons' house for a victory celebration. Excitement was still in the air. The guys were congratulating Dave and Sky by slapping five and rapping jive.

Sarah dumped chips and pretzels into bowls while Tasha made a huge bowl of veggie dip. They enlisted Allison to hand out sodas and juice to the crowd.

Sarah walked into the middle of the living room,

where Sky was standing with Cindy Phillips, José Melendez, and Kwame. "Sky, you sure woke up a tired game."

"Hey, lady," Kwame said, "that was not a tired game. My man Dave here hustled all night long." He went over to the CD player to put on some music.

"Thanks, Kwame," Dave murmured. "Everybody worked hard. It's a solid team."

Sky shook his head. "When I came to Murphy, they told me you had a pretty good team. Now I see that most of the team is my man Dave here."

"Wrong," Dave said. This time there was an edge to his voice. "Like I just said, Sky, everyone contributed tonight."

An awkward silence filled the room. Then Sky shrugged.

"Yeah, okay. If you say so."

"At least we won the game," Cindy Phillips said. "Now let's talk about something else."

Sarah felt grateful to her best friend for speaking up. Things had gotten pretty tense, and she wanted everyone to celebrate Murphy's victory, not argue about the team.

"Hey, Kwame," someone yelled. "The music has stopped. You're going to lose your reputation as a master deejay!"

Kwame smiled. "Not in your lifetime I won't," he said, and went back to sorting through the CD's.

José walked over to Sarah. "I noticed that you

have a stack of newspapers in your recycling bin. Do you know if you have the paper with the article that Mr. Cintron asked us to bring to class?"

"What article is that?" Tasha asked.

"Mr. Cintron asked us to find an article in last week's newspaper about some constitutional amendment that's been hanging around for two hundred years or so," Sarah said. "I cut it out of the paper last Sunday. I have it someplace, I hope," she added as she went to the bottom of the stairs, got her backpack, and started rummaging through it.

"I figured if anybody would be on top of it," José said, "it would be Sarah."

Sky watched Sarah fish out the clipping. "We didn't have all this homework at my last school," Sky said. "What a major drag, man."

"It's not so bad when you get used to it," Jennifer said. "In fact, sometimes it's even fun."

Sky shook his head. "You really think old newspapers are what's happening?" he asked. "I mean, you really think this talking about what's printed in the papers is going to get you over?"

"Might not get you over," Tasha said. "But it will definitely get you by history."

Sarah carried the article back into the room.

Allison handed Kwame a can of root beer. "So what's the big deal about the Constitution?" she asked. "It sure can't be as much fun as basketball."

"It's a bigger deal than a basketball game, that's

16

for sure," Kwame answered.

"Oh, you can't believe that. The Constitution? What was that, anyway? Some piece of paper that some old dudes wrote a long time ago," Sky said.

"Yeah, 1787 to be exact," said Kwame. "It protects our rights," he explained to Allison.

Sky smirked. "What did they know about rights?" He paused. "But I like that rap about the pursuit of happiness."

"Actually, that was the Declaration of Independence," said Jennifer.

"The what?" Sky looked confused. "Who cares," he went on. "Hey, why are we doing homework when we should be partying?"

"Hey, Sky," Jennifer said, "it's not going to change our lives, but that's what you've got to study if you want to make it in school—that's why they call it school*work*."

"Yeah, let me check it out." Sky grabbed the article from Sarah, nearly tearing it, and looked it over.

"It says here that parties should not be ruined by old newspaper articles—and that thirty-five states are about to rate, er, rate-ify, whatever, the amendment."

Sky suddenly looked annoyed. He crumpled the article and threw it at Kwame. "Here, Kwame, you're the brainiac."

Kwame didn't say a word. Instead he handed the ball of paper to Sarah. She smoothed it out, then glanced at Tasha and April. Sky certainly had a different perspective, she thought.

Sarah turned back to José. "I'll make a copy of it over the weekend and give it to you on Monday before class."

José took it from her. "No, I'll do that for you. You helped me. Let me return the favor."

"Sure." Sarah smiled back at José. "No problem."

Mr. and Mrs. Gordon got home just as April was leaving with Steve Adams. Sarah suspected that April and Steve were interested in each other. It had seemed that way since they'd performed together in Murphy High's version of *Romeo and Juliet*.

"How did the game go?" Mrs. Gordon asked.

"We kicked a little butt," Jennifer said.

"We?" Dave looked at Jennifer. "I didn't see you out on the court."

"It's like a collective 'we,' " Jennifer said. "Murphy High kicked butt."

"Sky, this is my Aunt Liz and my Uncle Donald," Tasha said.

"I've heard a lot about you," Donald Gordon said. "Congratulations on your win tonight."

"Hey, it was a team thing," Sky said, looking at Dave.

When everyone left, Tasha and Sarah started cleanup. It was at times like this, when they were alone together, that Sarah felt happiest to have her cousin living with her. Tasha's parents had died in a terrible car accident, and since then Tasha had spent time with several different relatives. Things had been a bit rough when Tasha first arrived at the Gordons', but now it almost seemed as if she'd always been there. And Tasha was becoming more at ease with Sarah's family every day.

"What did you think of Sky tonight?" Tasha asked.

Sarah made a face. "I think he acted like a jerk when he was here," she said, "but he's terrific on the court."

Tasha nodded, then was silent for a moment. "Did you notice the way he read that newspaper article?" she asked.

"I noticed him snatch it out of my hand, if that's what you mean."

Tasha shook her head. "No. I meant when he said that thirty-five states had to 'rate' the amendment."

"Maybe he meant to say 'ratify' and just made a mistake. He was tired; it was a hard game."

Tasha shrugged. "I don't know," she said, "it just seems like an odd mistake."

Three

"Morning, folks," Sarah said as she stumbled into the kitchen early on Monday. Mrs. Gordon, Tasha, and Allison were sitting in the kitchen.

"Girl, you were doing some heavy sleeping last night!" Tasha said. "I came in to ask you a question and you were dead to the world." Sarah took a glass down from one of the cabinets and poured orange juice into it.

"Check out the paper." Tasha handed her cousin a copy of *The Madison Advocate*. "Sports page."

Sarah thumbed through the paper until she found the sports section. She had decided that Tasha's interest in sports was a little strange, even if her father had been a professional football player. Sarah almost never read the sports pages.

21

"Wow! 'The Sky's the Limit for Murphy High Basketball.' " Sarah read the headline aloud.

"Yeah, but get to this." Tasha pointed to the long article underneath it. "It's all about how Sky is the best thing that ever happened to local basketball. I wonder how the other players are going to feel."

Sarah nodded, thinking about Dave in particular. "Maybe they'll be glad just to have a shot at the championship," she said. "Sky could turn an average season into a winning one."

Mrs. Gordon stood up. "It's time for me to get to the office," she said. "Have a good day, everyone."

Sarah, Tasha, and Allison all said good-bye as Mrs. Gordon went out the door.

"Sky looked pretty good on Friday," Tasha said, "but I'd like to see him go up against Dave."

Sarah suddenly noticed the time. "Let's get out of here before we're all late."

Four kids on the bus were reading the article about Sky. Sarah had a feeling that they'd be hearing a lot about Sky Hodges today.

In front of the school, Debbie Smith was talking to a group of girls. Debbie, a senior, had won the Miss Teen Madison pageant last year. Some of the boys thought she was hot stuff, but Sarah's opinion was that she was stuck on herself.

Usually Sarah didn't pay much attention to Debbie. But today Debbie was gushing so loudly that Sarah couldn't avoid hearing every word.

22

"Sky is the greatest thing that's happened to Murphy since I've been here," Debbie said.

"That's why we have to start a booster squad," another girl said.

Sarah groaned. "Did you hear that?"

"Airheads," Tasha said. "They're airheads, Sarah. I don't spend time with girls who have nothing better to do than start a booster club. I have to get to my locker. I'll catch you at lunchtime."

"See you later, cousin."

Just then José walked up. He was smiling. "Hi, Sarah. Here's the article. I made a copy and read it yesterday. But I'm not sure about some of the facts in it. Maybe we can go over it before class."

"Sure." Sarah smiled and took the clipping.

All morning the school was buzzing with comments about "the amazing Sky Man." In the halls between classes all the talk was about his height, gold chains, flamboyant style on and off the court, self-confidence, and, most of all, how he was going to keep Murphy in the news and in the basketball finals. Both times Sarah spotted him in the hallway, he was surrounded by high fives and smiles. He had definitely become Murphy's new hero.

At lunchtime, Sarah took her tray to the table where she always sat with her friends. Jennifer was already there, picking at a small salad. Sarah had a hunch that Jennifer was dieting for Sky's benefit.

"So have you actually seen the great Sky today?"

Sarah asked wryly. "Is he in any of your classes?"

"Coach Green has had him in the gym most of the day," said Jennifer.

Sarah eyed her friend suspiciously. "Oh, yeah? And how would you know?" she asked.

"Because I watched him practice for a while after homeroom." Jennifer sighed. "Girl, what he can do on that court is just unbelievable. And he is so tall, dark, and handsome."

Tasha sat down with her tray full of salad and fruit. "Hi, everyone." She turned to Jennifer. "Nice blouse."

"Thanks," Jennifer replied. "I got it yesterday at Ms. Tique in Westcove. I've always liked hot pink and Sky said he loved the gold collar."

Sarah and Tasha exchanged glances. "Pardon me, girlfriend," Sarah said, "but you forgot to mention that you actually *spoke* to Sky."

Jennifer blushed. "Well, I just wanted to know what he was into besides basketball."

"Uh-huh, and what did you find out?" Tasha asked, trying not to smile.

"Well, he's actually a very serious guy," Jennifer said defensively.

"Yeah, we saw how serious he was about school last night."

Jennifer ignored Tasha's comment. "He told me that he wants to apply to Georgetown and maybe four or five other colleges next year. But he really expects colleges to come to him. So he's talking to Coach Green about how to negotiate for the best deal."

"I bet he's got it all figured out already," Tasha said under her breath.

"What did you say?" asked Jennifer.

"Oh, never mind." Tasha took a big bite of an apple.

Cindy and April joined them. "Jennifer," Cindy said, "I just heard from an unnamed source that you were seen smiling your best smile up in Sky's face."

Sarah watched April try to look innocent. "Ahem, could the so-called 'unnamed source' be April Winter?" she asked.

They all laughed as they looked at April. She just shrugged. "Well, sure. When I walked past the gym before my first class, I saw Jennifer hanging out in the doorway watching Sky practice. And when I went by before second class, they were standing there talking."

This time everyone looked at Jennifer.

"Well, I . . . uh . . . kind of like him," Jennifer admitted.

"You 'kind of like him'?" Sarah said, raising an eyebrow. "You have a new blouse, you're eating salad for lunch, and you just tried to convince us how serious he is. Now you're telling us you just 'kind of like' Sky?"

Before Jennifer could answer, Dave Hunter came

over and sat down. He groaned. "Are you ladies still going on about my man Sky? He's all anybody's talking about today."

"Actually, Jennifer was just telling us how Sky expects colleges to be beating a path to his door," explained Sarah. "And before you know it, he'll be recruited for the NBA." Sarah was sorry for Dave. She thought about how he must feel, after all his hard work, being overshadowed after just one game.

"Dave, you know him better than any of us, right?" asked Tasha. "You think he's a big college player?"

"I think he's got it," Dave said.

"You've got it, too, Dave," Sarah blurted out. As soon as she said it, she wished she could take it back. She'd sounded too protective, as if they were a real couple. Dave squirmed in his seat and Sarah looked away.

Four

"Where's Miss Essie?" Sarah asked Allison as the two of them set the table for dinner. "Does she have an audition tonight?"

When Miss Essie had been widowed eight years ago, she had come to live with the Gordons. Now Sarah was used to having her grandmother around for dinner. Even though Miss Essie was an actress who still did some television work, she was almost always home at night.

Allison had a big grin on her face. "Miss Essie's out."

"Out where?" asked Sarah.

Allison paused dramatically. "Miss Essie went out on a *date*," she said.

"Get out of here!"

27

"She ran into this man she knows at an audition for a commercial," Allison explained. "He's an actor. They were both trying out for parts."

"And who is he?" asked Sarah.

Tasha came into the dining room. "Who is who?"

"I think she said his name was Gerard Taylor," said Allison.

"Gerard Taylor? That name sounds familiar," said Tasha.

"Yeah, Miss Essie told us about him once—he did some TV show or commercial," said Sarah.

"Do you know that bus commercial?" Allison asked. "The one with the woman who's sleeping and then the bus driver wakes her up and tells her that she's home?"

Tasha and Sarah nodded.

"Well, the bus driver is the guy who's taking Miss Essie out," Allison said, proud that she had remembered. "She was looking sharp," she went on. "She had on her blue silk dress and those cute little shoes she likes."

"Did Dad see all this?" Sarah asked.

Allison giggled. "Sure, but I don't think he liked it much."

"Yeah, it must be really strange seeing your mother go out on a date," Tasha said.

"Well, the way Miss Essie was smiling in Mr. Taylor's face, I think Dad had better get used to having him around," said Allison.

The phone rang. Mrs. Gordon answered it in the kitchen. "Sarah, it's José!" she called into the dining room.

Sarah went into the kitchen and picked up the phone. "Hello?"

"Hi," José said. "I just wanted to thank you again for helping me with that assignment. The article made a big difference in class."

"No problem," said Sarah. "I think we were the only ones in the class who looked that article up. Mr. Cintron was impressed."

"Sarah," said José.

"Yes?"

"I really like being your friend," said José. "Did you . . . did you find a note in your backpack?"

The note flashed into Sarah's mind. With all this stuff about Sky going on, she'd almost forgotten about it. "Yes, I found it." She took a deep breath.

"Well, I wrote it," José said. "When I saw you today, I realized that I can't keep it a secret anymore. I can't even wait until I see you tomorrow. I just have to say what I feel in my heart. Sarah, I love you."

Sarah was stunned. She let the phone slip from her ear.

"Sarah? Are you there?" asked José.

"José, I . . . I'm glad we're friends, too," she said, bringing the phone back up to her ear, "but maybe we should talk about this some other time. How about we meet tomorrow at 18 Pine?"

"Okay, it's a date. I'll meet you there after school." José's voice was a deep whisper on the phone. "Good night, my love."

At dinnertime, Sarah was still thinking about José's call. She'd known him for more than two years, and now they hung out together all the time at 18 Pine. She couldn't believe he'd been the one to leave the note. When her father asked her why she was so quiet, she looked up, startled. "Um . . . I'm trying to figure out what I'm going to write for my English assignment."

Mr. Gordon was the principal at Hamilton High, a high school in Madison for kids who needed extra attention and structure. He accepted Sarah's excuse that she was figuring out her homework assignment without a second thought. Tasha, however, was not fooled. She'd seen the change that had come over Sarah after her conversation with José.

After dinner, Tasha poked her head into Sarah's room. Sarah was just sitting on the bed. "So, are you going to invite me in or what?" Tasha asked.

"Come on in and close the door," said Sarah.

"Oh, wow. This must be serious," said Tasha as she dropped down on Sarah's bed. "You okay?"

"I don't know," said Sarah.

"Hey, cuz, I've never seen you like this before. What's up?"

"Remember the note I got? The one we thought

might have come from Kwame?"

"Yeah?"

"It wasn't Kwame, it was José!"

Tasha looked surprised. "José wrote the note? He's been a part of the gang for as long as I've been here—and I never even guessed he was interested in you."

"On the phone he told me that he loves me," Sarah said.

"He what?" Tasha practically yelled.

"Do you have a problem with José?" Sarah asked defensively.

"With those big, dark eyes? And those long eyelashes that go up and down when he's thinking?" Tasha shook her head.

Sarah grinned. "That's not what I meant. I was talking about the fact that he's Hispanic."

"You're right," Tasha said, "he *is* Hispanic—and he's fine! That's what it's all about." She grinned. "When I lived in Los Angeles I dated this guy named Juan. He was Mexican and looked a little like José. We had some good times."

"What happened?" Sarah asked. "Did it work out?"

Tasha smiled. "It was great. I got to practice my Spanish and I learned a lot about people that I never would have known if I hadn't dated him . . ." Her voice trailed off.

"So what happened?" repeated Sarah.

"Everything was going great with us. I think I might have even loved him. Maybe he loved me, too. But then I had to move—when my parents—" Tasha grew quiet.

Sarah moved across the bed and hugged Tasha. She was always aware that her cousin carried around the pain of losing both her parents in the car accident. But Sarah hadn't known until today that when she had left home, Tasha had also had to leave behind a boyfriend. Sometimes it seemed there were a lot of things about Tasha that she still didn't know.

Tasha pulled away from Sarah and looked at her cousin closely. "Sarah, how do *you* feel about José? And what about Dave? Are you giving up on him?"

"I don't know what to do about Dave," said Sarah. "I really like him, but he—we—just can't seem to make the decision to go ahead. I'm tired of waiting. I like José. He's fun to be around and I like talking to him. I just never thought of being his girlfriend. I'm black and he's Hispanic. I never thought . . . "

"Yeah, I know," Tasha said. "You never thought you could go out with a guy who wasn't African-American. But if you like him, none of that really matters. Why don't you let whatever has to happen, just happen? Then check it out. If you don't want a relationship with him, don't have one. A date isn't a lifelong commitment, you know."

Sarah thought about that for a minute. It made a

lot of sense. "How come you're so logical about all this?" she asked.

Tasha grinned as she stood up. "I'm not the one who has to deal with José," she said. "It's easy to be logical about somebody else's problems." She ducked as Sarah flung a pillow right at her head.

The next day Sarah was thinking about Tasha's advice as she entered 18 Pine St. to meet José. But when she saw Kwame, April, Cindy, Jennifer, and Tasha at their regular table, and José sitting alone near the back, Sarah felt queasy. How could she explain to her friends why she was walking past them to sit with José? Why had she suggested meeting at 18 Pine in the first place? Everyone would assume they were going out before Sarah had a chance to make up her own mind.

Before she could figure out what to do, Kwame called out, "Hey, Sarah. Where are you going?"

"Get over here," Jennifer chimed in. "Do you know what Sky told me today?"

"I have to talk to José about a history assignment," Sarah mumbled. "I'll check you out later. Don't eat *everything*."

Tasha hid her hand behind her napkin and gave Sarah a thumbs-up.

Sarah knew she was looking good. She had on her blue turtleneck and short black skirt. She had polished her nails a soft pink that morning and curled her hair along the sides of her face to show off her deep brown eyes.

She wasn't surprised when José commented on her appearance. What did surprise her was the fact that her heart skipped a beat at his words.

"I'm glad you came, Sarah," he said.

"Me too," she answered, smiling at him.

"I'll get some slices and sodas," he said. "Okay?"

"Great," Sarah answered. While she waited for him to return, she glanced back at her friends.

They knew something was going on—April wasn't even trying to pretend that she wasn't watching them. At least Dave isn't here today, Sarah thought. He'd probably hear about this from somebody—but it wasn't as if he was dying to go out with her. These days he barely seemed interested.

When José came back to their table with the slices and soda, he sat down opposite Sarah and took her hand.

"Well, did you think about what I told you last night?" he asked.

Sarah hesitated. "Yes. I like being your friend, José. I'm just not sure about anything else."

"Okay, then let's be friends. Good friends." He kissed Sarah's hand just as April walked past on her way to the rest room. Sarah slid down in her seat. April was sure to spread the news of José's kiss all over school.

34

Maybe she shouldn't have agreed to come today. But José was nice and very cute. Sarah sighed. What was she going to do?

18 PINE

Five

"Sarah, check this out," Dave yelled across the hallway. He held up a copy of *The Madison Advocate* for her to see the headline: "Sky's the Limit".

Sarah walked over to him. "You know Tasha—she reads the sports pages every morning. There's no chance I'd miss a headline like that with her around."

Dave laughed. "Having Sky on the team is pretty good publicity for Murphy—and we may actually get somewhere this season. He's a pain sometimes, but I guess I can live with him. They're having a rally this afternoon. You going to be there?"

"Sure," Sarah answered, wondering why Dave seemed interested in where she was going all of a sudden.

"Okay," Dave said. "I'll see you at the gym."

By the time Sarah got to the gym, it was packed. It looked as if there were even more people at this rally than there had been at the game on Saturday. Tasha waved Sarah over to where she was sitting with Jennifer, Cindy, and April.

"Look over there across the court," Sarah said. "Debbie and her boosters got their T-shirts."

"Is that gross or what?" Jennifer said. "Silly looking pink T-shirts. They could have at least gotten the school colors. Or maybe bothered to match their shirts with their socks. Those purple socks just have to go."

Coach Green came out on the court in a Murphy High sweatshirt, his large stomach stretching the shirt tight. The crowd cheered and threw confetti as he signaled for the team to stand. The six boosters started chanting, "Go Sky! Go Sky!" and shaking their pom-poms. The crowd joined in. Sky, who was standing next to Dave, smiled broadly at all the attention. He was obviously loving it.

Mr. Green motioned for the crowd to be quiet. The players sat down. "I'm going to keep this short and sweet," the coach began. "We are winners! Every time Murphy's basketball team wins, the whole school wins with us. We're making our presence felt in Madison."

A group of students interrupted, yelling, "Yes! Yes!"

"Now I want to introduce you to Mr. Tommy Rivera," the coach went on. "Mr. Rivera, will you please stand up?"

A large man in a light gray suit stood up in the front row. He smiled nervously. Coach Green continued, "We are proud to have Mr. Rivera here with us today. He is a Murphy graduate and a leading citizen of Madison. He now owns his own car dealership over on Water Street. He was also a star player on our basketball team."

Mr. Rivera looked a little uneasy as the crowd cheered. He probably isn't used to getting so much attention, Sarah thought. Two students rolled a big cart onto the court. On it was a large object covered with a cloth.

When the crowd quieted, Coach Green spoke again. "Mr. Rivera has been so impressed by our winning lineup that he has honored Murphy with the donation of this brand-new overhead projector for our Media Center."

The crowd cheered as the coach took the cloth off the projector. "To show our appreciation to Mr. Rivera, we're giving him season tickets." Coach Green handed Mr. Rivera an envelope and shook his hand.

"I've had enough of this jock stuff," Kwame said to Sarah. "Whenever a team starts to do well, all the alumni start supporting the school. Where are they when we win a science fair or a math contest? Let's split."

"Good move," Sarah said. "If we wait till the end, with all this crowd, we'll never get out of here."

"See you later," Jennifer said. "I want to stay and watch Sky."

"I'll hang out, too," Tasha added. "See you later, cousin."

When Sarah got home at five, her mother was already there getting dinner ready. This was unusual. Most of the time Sarah and Tasha were home before Mrs. Gordon.

"Easy day, Mom?" Sarah asked.

Her mother smiled. "Yes, and it feels great to be home early for a change. Makes up for some of those late nights. Want to give me a hand with dinner? Miss Essie's out again."

Sarah put her books down and took some salad greens out of the refrigerator. As she washed them, she chatted with her mother.

"So where's Miss Essie going tonight?"

"Out with Mr. Taylor again," Mrs. Gordon replied. "They were going to Jimmy's for the early-bird special."

Sarah grinned. "Hey, fancy schmancy."

"She does seem to like him," Mrs. Gordon replied. "She looked beautiful when she left."

Sarah set plates around the dining room table, then returned to the kitchen for silverware. She saw her mother smiling at her.

"Thanks, honey," Mrs. Gordon said. "You know, I

miss having time alone with you. It's been a while since it was just the two of us, hasn't it?"

Impulsively Sarah reached over to hug her mother. "I love you, Supermom," she said with tears in her eyes. "It's great having you home." It had been a while since they'd been alone. Sarah loved having Tasha living with them, but sometimes she missed the old days when it was just Sarah, Allison, and their mother and father.

"So tell me what's new at school," Mrs. Gordon said as the two of them went back to their chores.

Sarah hesitated. She wanted to tell her mother about José and how confused she felt about him and about Dave. She was trying to find the words when Tasha burst through the front door. "Hey, Sarah," she called out. "You missed the best part."

"What happened?" Sarah asked.

Tasha rolled her eyes. "The airheads on the pep squad did a few cheers. The entire gym was calling Sky's name over and over. Too bad they don't realize that sports are about doing your best, not about winning." She scowled. "And of course Jennifer waited to meet Sky when he left school."

"You and I have had enough of Sky, but it looks like Jennifer is just getting started," Sarah said.

"That's for sure," Tasha agreed. "Sometimes that girl has a good head on her shoulders. Other times . . . "

Sarah grinned. "I know what you mean."

*   *   *

41

Just as the Gordons were finishing dinner, Miss Essie's key turned in the lock. She seemed to float into the dining room. "Good evening, everyone," she said. Mr. Taylor was with her. Miss Essie had her arm linked in his.

Mr. Taylor was about Miss Essie's age, with slicked-back black hair and a pencil-thin mustache. His skin was the brownish-gray color of tree trunks. He was wearing a 1950s-style blue pinstriped suit. Sarah thought he was handsome in an old-fashioned way.

Miss Essie introduced him to Tasha and Sarah and Mr. Gordon, then said, "Gerard and I have had such a wonderful time this evening that I wanted him to spend some time getting to know all of you." She beamed at Mr. Taylor.

Mrs. Gordon stood up. "Let's move into the living room. Mr. Taylor, would you like some coffee?"

"How lovely of you to ask. Yes, I would like a cup, thank you," he replied.

Tasha and Sarah finished clearing the table while Mrs. Gordon made coffee. As the others headed into the living room, Sarah heard her father speak to Mr. Taylor. "You've known each other a long time, haven't you?"

"That's right," Mr. Taylor replied. "I think we met in 1947." He reached for Miss Essie's hand as they sat together on the sofa.

"Did you see that, Tasha?" Sarah said with a giggle. "The two of them are acting like kids our age."

"Uncle Donald doesn't seem to like it much," Tasha replied.

Sarah looked at her father. Tasha was right. His smile seemed glued to his face and he was speaking in stiff, awkward tones.

Sarah and Tasha loaded the dishwasher, then joined the others. They both sat cross-legged on the floor. Mr. Taylor looked at them, then smiled at Miss Essie.

"Sweetheart, should we talk about it now?" he asked. Miss Essie nodded.

"Well, then, it's all very simple," Mr. Taylor said. "I love Essie Gordon and want to marry her."

"And I'm strongly considering the possibility," Miss Essie added.

Mr. Gordon practically choked on his coffee. Allison stifled a giggle and Sarah could feel her own mouth drop open.

"A wedding. How wonderful." Mrs. Gordon was the first to speak. She went over to the sofa to hug Miss Essie. "We're happy for both of you."

Sarah watched her father struggle to regain his composure. He stood up. "Yes, Mother, if that's really what you want to do . . ."

"I want to be a bridesmaid," Sarah said.

"Hey, me too," Tasha managed to say. "And Allison can be the flower girl."

Miss Essie squeezed Mr. Taylor's hand. "We

don't want to rush into anything. I've told Gerard I need a little time to get used to the idea. But so far, I like it."

As Miss Essie and Mr. Taylor chattered away happily about their plans, Mr. Gordon was silent. Finally he reached over to shake Mr. Taylor's hand. "If you'll excuse me, I have some work to prepare for tomorrow."

Sarah and Tasha exchanged glances. Later, when they were alone in Sarah's room, they talked about Mr. Gordon's strong reaction.

"Well, Dad may not like Mr. Taylor much," Sarah said, "but Miss Essie sure seems to be happy with him."

Tasha nodded. Then she said, "I don't know what it is, but there's something strange about that guy."

Sarah looked her cousin in the eye. "That's exactly what I was thinking," she said.

PINE

Six

"Tasha!"

Tasha stopped walking down the front steps of Murphy High and turned. Steve and April were coming toward her. April looked upset.

"What's up?" Tasha asked as they reached her.

"Steve overheard a discussion in the office today," April began. "He was just standing there and—"

"See you two around," Steve interrupted. "I've got to get home. I . . . uh . . . have a lot of homework tonight. April can tell you what happened."

"Good luck with it . . . " Tasha started to say, but Steve was already gone.

"Must be a whole lot of homework," she commented, turning to April. "I've never seen Steve take off so fast."

"I don't think he really has that much homework," April admitted. "He was just using that as an excuse to get out of here."

Now Tasha was really baffled. "What's going on?"

"Well, hey—did you see Sarah and José looking at each other in lunch today?" April said, interrupting herself.

"Tell me about what Steve heard," Tasha said, trying to get April back on the topic.

"Steve happened to be in the office today when Mr. Miller, the college counselor, came in," April explained. "And he heard him saying that he'd just gotten Bill Hodges's scores for his Scholastic Aptitude Test."

"Bill Hodges?" Tasha asked. "Who's that?"

"That's Sky's real name," April said. "And he said that his test scores were, like, miserable. They were five hundred! Total!"

"That doesn't surprise me too much," Tasha replied. "Remember when he came to our house after the game? And he was looking at that article that Sarah and José were interested in?"

"Yeah," April said.

"Well, he said that thirty-five states had to 'rate' the amendment before it became a part of the Constitution. The paper said that thirty-five states had to 'ratify' the amendment. I'm not sure he can even read that well."

"Really?" April's eyes widened.

"I thought maybe I was wrong, but with his test scores . . . I think you get four hundred on that test if you just write your name down." Tasha shook her head.

"To make matters worse," April said, "there was this other kid in the office and he heard about the scores, too. He made a remark—that's why Steve didn't want to tell you about it."

"You're not really clearing things up here, April," Tasha said.

The younger girl looked embarrassed. "He was just some jerk. He said that Sky was nothing but a stupid ape and he should go back to the jungle he came from," she blurted out. "That's what made Steve mad. It made him mad and it embarrassed him, too. Steve and I aren't hung up about being the only white kids in the gang, but sometimes it gets awkward."

Tasha shook her head. "There are a lot of ignorant people in the world, April, but you and Steve aren't among them. You didn't say anything. Steve didn't say anything."

"Well, anyway," April went on, "Mr. Miller called Sky down to the office and told him what his test scores meant."

"How did he take it?"

"It really didn't seem to faze him at all," April answered. "Steve said he told Mr. Miller that the scores don't matter. According to Sky, with his talent in basketball, any college will want him. He went out smiling and swaggering just like he was doing when he came in."

"He just might be right," Tasha said, half to herself. "Look, April, I'll see you later."

When Tasha arrived later that afternoon at 18 Pine St., Sarah was telling Jennifer, Kwame, and Billy Turner about Miss Essie's engagement. Tasha sat down at their table and tore off a piece of Sarah's pizza.

"Wait a minute. You mean that old lady is getting married?" Billy said.

"Say *what*?" Sarah's voice rose sharply.

Billy Turner played on the basketball team with Dave, and he often hung out at 18 Pine with the gang. He had dated Sarah a few times, until she had discovered that he already had a girlfriend. Later he had gone out with Tasha, making him one of the only boys to have dated both of the cousins. After forgiving him for being a jerk, Sarah had actually started to like him. But right now, she was annoyed at him.

"I didn't mean it the way it sounded," Billy mumbled.

"My grandmother may be in her seventies," Sarah fired back, "but she's a working actress who probably has more energy than all of us combined.

48

Besides, whatever her age is, she has the right to get married, if it makes her happy."

"I didn't say—"

"And furthermore," Sarah interrupted, "whatever she decides to do is her business and not ours." Sarah still had misgivings about Miss Essie's "engagement," but she didn't want anyone—especially Billy Turner—making fun of her grandmother's decision.

"Hey, there's Sky," Billy said, nodding toward the door.

"Can't we ever discuss anything without having him or some talk about him interrupt us?" Kwame mumbled.

Tasha turned. As Sky entered, several people called out greetings and gave him high fives. He stopped to talk to Jimmy Caitlin, another basketball player, and then he spotted Jennifer across the room.

As Sky headed toward their table, a frown crossed Kwame's face. "Great way to ruin a friendly conversation," he muttered.

Jennifer glared at him.

"Come on, Kwame, lighten up," Billy said. "Sky's all right."

"Are you jealous or something?" Jennifer asked.

Kwame didn't respond. Instead he watched in silence as the new player stood behind Jennifer and rubbed her shoulders. "How's my girl?" Sky asked.

Jennifer sighed deeply. "Fine now," she said.

"Oh, spare us," Kwame said under his breath.

Sky didn't appear to have heard him. He pulled a chair up to the table and flopped into it. "So what's up?" he said.

"Grab a chair, Sky," Tasha said.

"When I look up," Jennifer said softly, "all I see is Sky."

"I hear that!" Sky said.

Kwame was eager to change the focus of the conversation. "Oh, I forgot to tell you guys," he said. "I'm buying those books I mentioned. The guy wants seventy dollars for them, but he's letting me pay him off ten dollars a week."

"What books are you talking about?" Sky asked.

"Kwame is into African-American history," Billy explained. "He's got this big collection of history books in his house."

"Yo, man." Sky shook his head, "You mean you're out there buying books you don't even need for school? You don't have anything better to do with your money?"

Kwame stared at him. "That's funny," he said. "I thought it was important to educate myself."

There was an uncomfortable silence as the two stared at each other, neither willing to look away first.

Jennifer shot Kwame a dirty look. Tasha nudged Sarah under the table.

"Hey," Sky said to Kwame. "What are you trying

to say, little man?"

"I spoke my piece," Kwame said. "It sounded clear to me."

"Don't try to dis me!" Sky's eyes narrowed.

"Later for you, Sky!" Kwame flipped his hand at the basketball star.

Sky shot straight up, knocking his chair over behind him. He towered above Kwame. For a moment he just glared downward. Then he seemed to remember Jennifer. He looked at her and said, "Pardon me, lady love, but we have a real fool here."

Kwame's face hardened. Sarah held her breath, praying her friend would just let the whole thing blow over. "If you'll excuse me," Kwame said, "I'd like to finish my pizza."

Sky broke out laughing. "You'd like to what? Folks, this is not just a fool, this is a lame fool. So, you'd like to finish your pizza, uh-huh."

Sky picked up a slice from Kwame's plate and shoved it toward Kwame's mouth. Kwame ducked.

Jennifer stood up. "Sky, leave him alone."

"Okay," Sky said finally, looking at Kwame. "This turkey's not worth it."

Kwame looked down at his plate, then pushed himself away from the table and got up to leave.

Sarah jumped up. "Wait, Kwame, I want to talk to you."

When he saw her walking after him, Kwame waited for her. Sarah grabbed his hand and led him to an empty booth in the back. When he sat down, he looked really shaken. Sarah had never seen him like this.

"So, Kwame," she said, "what's going on with you and Sky?"

"You saw what happened. You know the deal," he said, looking away.

"Why did you start with Sky in the first place?" she asked.

"Because I don't like his attitude."

"Well, neither do I. But I'm smart enough not to bother him about it."

"Look, Sarah, you don't understand. It's a male thing," he countered.

"But I want to understand," Sarah said. "We're friends, right?"

Kwame nodded and smiled.

"Well, tell me about it."

Kwame sighed. "You know how hard I work to keep my grades up. It's important to me. My parents tell me all the time how hard it can be for black people to get ahead and how much it counts for me to do well in school."

"Sure, I know that. My father's a principal. He tells me that all the time. I work pretty hard at it myself. And so does Tasha."

"Yeah, I know. But it's different for girls," he said.

"And how so?" she demanded.

"You don't have to sit in Mr. Cala's class when he calls out Sky's name," Kwame said, looking down again. "You see, it's like whenever Sky can't do the work, he's showing me up to everyone in that class who isn't black. They see one black kid who's getting by because he can play ball and they assume we all are. I don't want to be seen that way."

"What? Kwame, everyone knows you're an A-plus student. For goodness sake, what does Sky have to do with you?" Sarah was confused.

"He is a black man. I am a black man. When a teacher sees me, he sees Sky. And I don't like what he sees," said Kwame. "And it kills me that Sky doesn't care at all. He thinks he can get by on his basketball abilities."

"Okay, I get it," said Sarah. "But that's no reason to pick on Sky."

Kwame shrugged. "I can't help it. He's really talented at basketball. I'm really talented in academics. It would be great if we all could be seen as individuals. But I'm not sure if the rest of the world can handle that."

"Maybe, Kwame, you're the one who can't handle it. You almost sound like you want Sky to be more like you. Let up. Let him be himself."

"Sarah, I know you're right, but it's so irritating." Kwame clenched his fist.

"Look, you can't take it personally when Sky screws up in school," said Sarah.

53

Kwame took a deep breath. "You're right, Sarah. I can't let him get to me so much."

Sarah smiled. "Good for you, Kwame. Now pick up your soda and let's go back there."

"What?"

"You heard what I said, man. Let's go back and show them you're still among the living," she said.

"Oh, all right."

When they got back to their usual table, Sky said, "Well, look what we have here. The return of the chump."

Kwame ignored him.

"Sky was telling us about his career plans," Jennifer said.

"His career?" Sarah asked. She wanted to say that Sky should be thinking first about graduating from high school.

"That's right," Tasha said. "Sky thinks he'll be a big star."

Sky didn't seem to notice Tasha's sarcastic tone. "Coach Green thinks I've got what it takes to hit the spotlights."

"That sounds great," said Steve.

Jennifer nodded. "I like a man who knows what he wants. And one who has the talent to make it happen."

"You'd better believe it," Sky continued. "I want money and power. And with my talent, I don't need to study any algebra problems to get it.

I've got my jump shot."

Somehow Sarah didn't feel so sure about Sky's future.

Seven

The Mount Vernon Colonials had beaten Murphy High for six years in a row. Three times they had gone on to win the upstate championship, and everyone was expecting a close game this year.

When José called on Friday to invite Sarah to the game the next day, she hesitated, then said yes. It wasn't really a date, she decided, since their other friends would be around, and they were only going to a basketball game. How romantic could that get?

Sarah sat in the stands with José and Tasha, watching the players warm up. When it was Sky's turn to practice lay-ups, he didn't do anything fancy. He just took the ball from Dave, moved in easily, and laid the ball against the backboard. It rolled along the rim and then fell through.

"Half the school is here," José said. "Even the teachers."

Sarah looked around and saw that there *were* a lot of teachers present. "I guess everyone's curious to see what all the excitement is about," she said, nodding toward Sky.

The players from Mount Vernon were wearing expensive white warm-up suits with their names embroidered on the chest. They looked good in their warm-up drills, and most of them were taller than the Murphy High players.

The game started with Mount Vernon scoring the first six points, two on outside shots and one on a slam dunk from their center. Sky missed an outside shot and Billy missed an easy lay-up.

Then, while Dave was shooting, a Mount Vernon player grabbed his shirt. Dave was awarded two foul shots and he easily hit both of them. It was Mount Vernon 6, Murphy 2.

José took off his jacket and laid it across his lap. Then he took Sarah's hand under the jacket so that no one could see them holding hands. Sarah smiled uneasily at him. This wasn't really what she'd had in mind when she'd told José she just wanted to be friends—but she liked the way her hand felt in his. And no one else seemed to notice.

As the game proceeded, Mount Vernon kept the lead. "Sky doesn't seem to be doing anything special," Sarah said. Her cousin agreed.

Dave was moving well with the ball and scored two easy baskets when the Mount Vernon team lost him under the boards. But the score was Mount Vernon 26, Murphy 17.

Dave tightened up his defense and Mount Vernon fought hard to score their next two baskets. At the end of the first half the score was Mount Vernon 33, Murphy 24.

The second half started with Murphy switching from a zone defense to a tough man-to-man.

"This is where we'll see it happen," Tasha said.

Billy spotted Sky on the side and passed the ball. It got to Sky a split second before the Mount Vernon player reached him. Sky took one step and went up for the shot. The Mount Vernon player went up with him. Sky spun in the air, turning in a complete circle before reaching over the Mount Vernon player to slam the ball through the net.

The Murphy High crowd roared. José jumped up and threw his hands in the air, forgetting for the moment that he was holding Sarah's hand.

Dave intercepted the in-bounds pass and went right to the basket. He made the lay-up and Sarah got the sense that Murphy was in charge. Murphy scored the next nine points to take the lead, with Sky in on every play. Mount Vernon called time out.

Sarah spotted Mr. Cala, the math teacher, in the stands with an older woman. She must be his mom,

Sarah thought, and snickered to herself. Sarah remembered how badly Mr. Cala had treated Tasha when he thought she'd cheated on a test—she wasn't surprised he didn't have any friends with him at the game. He was usually in a bad mood, but today even he seemed caught up in the excitement of the game.

Sarah watched the game, and she was glad to see Dave doing so well, but she had a hard time getting excited about the finer points of basketball. It seemed like a bunch of tall guys sweating a lot.

Finally there was only one minute left in the game. Billy started a play from deep in the Murphy end. He threw a long pass. Sky went up, caught the ball, and threw it out to Dave. Dave started downcourt, slowed at the top of the key, then threw a lob pass. It was Sky who caught the ball on the palm of his hand and stuffed it through the basket. The game was over, and Murphy had finally beaten Mount Vernon.

"The guy's fantastic!" José said as he walked with Sarah toward the bus stop. "He's got everything—the size, the right moves, and the touch."

As José rehashed the exciting plays, Sarah kept an eye out for Dave. She still wasn't sure how she felt about José, or Dave for that matter, and she didn't want to deal with a confrontation.

"Here comes your bus," Sarah said. "I'm going to

catch up with Tasha. See you later?"

"Yeah, sure," José said. "Look, you think we can go out this week?"

Before she could decide what to say, she heard herself blurt out, "It's early still. Why don't you come over for supper tonight?" As soon as she said it, she felt relieved. At least she wasn't stalling him.

"When do you want me to come over?" José asked.

"About seven," Sarah said. "Now go catch your bus."

José lifted Sarah's hand and kissed it gently. Then he put his fingers under her chin and lifted her mouth to his. His body was touching hers as lightly as his lips were touching her mouth.

Before Sarah could stop herself, she put her arms around him and kissed him back. For a second, it felt as if they were alone in the world. Finally Sarah opened her eyes and gently pushed José toward his bus. "I'll see you later," she whispered.

She was confused about José, but she decided not to worry about it right now. She wanted to enjoy the feeling. She caught up with Tasha, who wanted to know where she and José had disappeared to after the game.

"You going to tell me about it?" Tasha asked.

"No," Sarah said. "I still can't figure it out for myself."

*　　*　　*

When Sarah and Tasha arrived home, Mr. Taylor was sitting on the living room sofa. He stood and bowed slightly.

"It's a pleasure to see you two lovely young ladies again," he said.

"Hi." Sarah smiled at him.

Tasha shook Mr. Taylor's hand politely. Sarah noticed she wasn't smiling. "Is Miss Essie around?" asked Tasha.

"Yes. She's talking with her son," he replied.

Sarah glanced at Tasha. Why was Miss Essie having a private conversation with Mr. Gordon? Did this mean that their grandmother had made up her mind about getting married?

Just then Miss Essie came into the living room. She was carrying a manila envelope.

"Here you go, Gerard," she said. "Hi, girls. How was the game?"

"Great," Tasha said. "We creamed them in the second half."

"Way to go," her grandmother replied.

Mr. Taylor took the envelope from Miss Essie, then put his arm around her. "Sweetheart, you don't know what this means to me. Thank you so much. I'll get it back to you in a few weeks."

"I know you will." Miss Essie smiled and kissed him on the cheek. Mr. Taylor picked up his hat and walked toward the door. "Good-bye, girls. I'll see you soon."

Before leaving, he kissed Miss Essie's lips. She closed the door and turned toward the girls. She was grinning and looked ten years younger to Sarah.

"So, Miss Essie, when's the wedding date?" asked Sarah.

"No date yet. Mr. Taylor has to clear up some business before we can set a date," she said.

Mr. Gordon spoke from the hallway behind Sarah. "So, Mother," he said, "you actually gave it to him."

"Yes, I actually did," Miss Essie said. "And I thank you for your concern."

Sarah thought the subject would die right there, but her father wasn't willing to let it drop. He turned to Tasha and Sarah. "Do you know what your grandmother did this afternoon? She went down to the bank, took out a large portion of what your grandfather left her, and just gave it to Mr. Taylor."

"Donald, please, don't be so anxious about everything," Miss Essie said. "And just to set the record straight, I *loaned* him the money. He just needs it for a few weeks."

There was an uncomfortable pause. Sarah had never seen her father and Miss Essie act so cold to one another. She decided to change the subject. "Dad, is it okay if a friend of mine comes to dinner tonight?"

Donald Gordon took his eyes from his mother and nodded to Sarah. The corners of his mouth were still tight. "What's her name?"

"Um . . . José." Sarah thought of his kiss and smiled.

"José? Really . . . " Tasha said.

"Do I know this young man?" Mr. Gordon raised his eyebrows.

"You will soon, Uncle Donald," Tasha said. "That's for sure."

José arrived at the Gordons' at ten minutes to seven. He was wearing a gray jacket, navy slacks, and a silk tie, with a crooked knot. Sarah was wearing a blue silk blouse—her favorite because it looked like a baseball jacket—and jeans. She greeted him at the door and led him to the living room. She was surprised at how nicely he was dressed.

"These are for you." José handed her a small bouquet of red roses.

"Thank you. They're beautiful." Sarah was thrilled. She started to take them to the kitchen to get water and a vase, but Mr. Gordon came into the living room.

"Aren't you going to introduce me to your friend?" Mr. Gordon asked with a grin. "He's so dressed up, I feel as if our butler should have answered the door."

Sarah smiled at José. "Dad, I would like you to meet my friend José. José, meet my father."

"Pleased to meet you, sir," José said, extending

his hand. "I've been waiting for a chance to meet the parents of such a special woman."

Mr. Gordon looked surprised as he shook José's hand. "We know she's special . . . "

"The roses are from José," Sarah said, trying to change the subject, then realizing at once how obvious it must look. José was blowing this dinner totally out of proportion—she started to get nervous about how the rest of the evening would go.

"Very nice." Mr. Gordon looked at the flowers briefly and then walked away.

Mrs. Gordon had put together a fabulous dinner of roast chicken, potatoes, a salad made by Tasha, and a chocolate cake baked by Sarah the day before.

José sat across from Sarah. He's trying so hard to have perfect manners, she thought. She decided that he *was* sort of cute. Every once in a while she would find herself looking into his eyes, and every time she did she smiled.

Throughout dinner, Mr. Gordon was very quiet, looking from Miss Essie to Sarah to José.

"What is it like being the principal at Hamilton?" José asked.

Mr. Gordon was clearly pleased at the question. "Challenging," he said. "The kids at Hamilton have everything it takes to make it in the real world— they just need a little extra time or attention to focus on the tasks at hand. It's very rewarding work."

Mrs. Gordon told José about her work as a lawyer,

and he seemed very interested. "My mother is a doctor," he said. "She has to spend a lot of time balancing her schedule in order to be around for my seven brothers and sisters. It's difficult sometimes."

Tasha looked at Sarah. They couldn't imagine having a house with that many kids.

When Sarah went to the door with José to say good night, she hoped he wouldn't try to kiss her.

"You have a great family," he said. "I can see why you're so terrific."

"Thanks," she answered. José had been great throughout the entire dinner, but she still felt a little uncomfortable.

José bowed, kissed her hand, and was gone.

When she closed the door and turned around, her father was standing across the room. "There's something about him . . . " he said.

Mrs. Gordon's brow furrowed. "What do you mean, Donald? He's a perfectly nice boy."

"I bet I know what it is," Sarah said.

"Oh, really." Mr. Gordon looked amused to hear that Sarah thought she could read his mind.

"I bet you don't like him because he's Hispanic," she blurted out.

"Nonsense! That is not it at all," her father said.

"What else could it be? He's one of the nicest boys I know!" Suddenly Sarah felt very angry at her father. "José is much more than a nice boy," she said. She was confused—she didn't feel ready to defend José to her father, yet she didn't want him to criticize him, either.

"Sarah," Mr. Gordon said, "your friend José is a nice boy with a nice smile. I just hope you're not too serious about him."

"I don't know why you don't like anything I do!" Sarah said. Her eyes filled with tears, and she went past her father toward the stairs.

"I know I don't like your melodrama, young lady!" her father called after her.

Tasha felt bad for her cousin. She couldn't see why Mr. Gordon didn't like José. Maybe Sarah was right, and Mr. Gordon was unhappy because José was Hispanic and not African-American. Tasha went in to help Miss Essie clean up the kitchen.

Sarah had fallen asleep across her bed. She felt someone sit down next to her and awakened to see Miss Essie by her side.

Miss Essie gave Sarah a big hug. "It's been a hard day around here for us ladies, hasn't it?"

"Miss Essie, why did Dad say that?" Sarah asked. "He doesn't know anything about José."

"Well, he does know one thing," Miss Essie replied with a grin.

Sarah was puzzled. "What?"

"He knows that José has a crush on his daughter."

Sarah turned away and blushed.

"First, I know that your father is not bothered by

the fact that José is Hispanic," Miss Essie continued. "Your father has always had friends of every race and every background," she said. "When he was growing up he used to bring just about anyone into the house. White, black, you name it. Now he's a principal at a school with all kinds of people. José's being Hispanic is not an issue at all."

"Then what is the problem?" Sarah asked her grandmother.

"The problem is very simple. José is a young man who seems interested in his daughter," Miss Essie said with a knowing smile.

"And I'm interested in him. So why—"

"And that makes your dad feel threatened," said Miss Essie. "He doesn't care if José is Hispanic or black or a Martian." Sarah smiled as Miss Essie continued. "The problem with José is that he's male. Your father knows that having boyfriends and dates is all part of your growing up, and that means he has to let go of you a little bit. It's not easy."

Sarah shrugged. "Maybe," she said. "But what about you—Dad was giving you a hard time today, too."

Her grandmother nodded. "He was angry that I lent my gentleman friend seven thousand dollars. It's my decision. It's a little risky to lend friends money, but life is full of risks."

"Well, lending somebody seven thousand dollars may be risky," Sarah said. "But I'm sure you know what you're doing. You must think he's nice."

"He is," Miss Essie said.

"And what do you think of José?"

"I didn't think they still made them that good-looking!" Miss Essie said with a laugh. "Now go downstairs and have a heart-to-heart with that father of yours."

Eight

On Monday, Sarah stayed at school a little late to do some research in the library. The halls were almost empty and the school was quiet when she went to her locker to get her books before meeting everyone at 18 Pine St.

As she rummaged through her books, she heard Mr. Cala arguing in an indignant tone from inside the math department office.

"I don't care about the basketball team."

"Listen to me," someone replied. It was Coach Green. "Sky Hodges is good for Murphy. A winning team attracts attention and donations and generates school pride."

"But what about Sky?" asked Mr. Cala. "The kid can barely add and subtract," he added icily.

"Look, Cala," answered the coach. "Sky doesn't have a chance to make it without basketball. If he plays well, he goes to college and then maybe makes a career out of it. If he doesn't play, he's on the street."

Sarah heard Mr. Cala sigh.

"Virtually every other teacher is on board. Just you and Mrs. Parisi." The coach continued, "You don't want to be known as the teacher who cost Murphy the season, do you?"

Sarah heard someone coming down the hall, so she quickly closed her locker and left. She couldn't believe it. It sounded as if Coach Green was bullying Mr. Cala into passing Sky. Wait until Tasha heard about this.

On the way home from 18 Pine St., Sarah filled her cousin in on what she'd overheard Coach Green saying to Mr. Cala at school.

Tasha shook her head. "That doesn't surprise me at all," she said. "The coach's only concern is that Sky plays and gets a win for his team. My father told me it happens to athletes all the time. No one has the guts to do what's best for the student."

"But that's terrible," Sarah said. "Isn't there anything we can do about it?"

Tasha shrugged. "He's got to decide to help himself first, Sarah."

When they got home at about five, they found

Mrs. Gordon trying to comfort Miss Essie, who was crying on the sofa. Mr. Gordon was pacing back and forth, looking very angry. The girls hurried past this upsetting scene and went to the kitchen, where Allison was eating from a box of cookies.

"What's going on?" Sarah asked.

"Shhh!" Allison put her finger to her lips. It was obvious she was eavesdropping.

Sarah and Tasha were too curious. They walked back toward the living room.

"I can't believe you let this happen," Mr. Gordon was saying.

"I didn't just let it happen," they heard Miss Essie answer.

"Well, if you hadn't given that scam artist your money . . . " Mr. Gordon said as Sarah and Tasha entered the room.

"What happened?" asked Tasha.

The three adults looked surprised to see the girls. Mrs. Gordon said calmly, "Your grandmother called me at work. It seems that Mr. Taylor has disappeared with Miss Essie's money. No one knows where he is or what he's done with the money. He's taken all of his furniture and left his apartment."

"Oh, no! What can we do?" asked Sarah.

"I'm trying to convince your grandmother to go to the police," Mr. Gordon said, "but she's being very stubborn about the whole thing."

"I have faith that Gerard will show up," Miss

Essie said, but Sarah thought she didn't look too confident. In her hand was a note, obviously from Mr. Taylor. Sarah could just read it. All it said was "Sorry."

"What gives you that faith, Mother?" Mr. Gordon demanded. "Just give me some evidence that backs up that faith."

"I don't have to give you evidence, Donald," Miss Essie shot back, fingering the note. "I may be an old woman, but I'm still capable of handling my own affairs."

"Yes, Mother, you are," Mr. Gordon said, speaking through clenched teeth. "But this time I think you've been taken advantage of."

"Now, just a minute, Donald," she said. "In retrospect, I agree that trusting Gerard might not have been the smartest thing I've ever done. In fact, it might have been downright foolish. But there is no one who is more upset than me. So I plan to do something about it."

Mr. Gordon shook his head in disbelief. "Oh, really. Like what?"

"Don't even ask. You'll see." With that, Miss Essie stood and marched to her room.

After dinner, Tasha and Allison sat down to watch television and Sarah decided to go to her room to finish her homework. She had wanted to talk to her father about José, just to make sure how he felt about her dating a Hispanic boy. Now, she thought, was definitely not the time.

The phone rang and someone picked it up. There was a pounding on Sarah's door, obviously Allison, and a second later her sister barged in.

"There's a phone call for you!"

"Hello?" Sarah said as she picked up the phone and Allison bounced out of the room again.

"Hey, how's it going?" Dave Hunter's voice said.

"Oh, hi, Dave," Sarah said as she sat down on the floor. She was pleased—and a little surprised—to hear from him. "What's up?"

"Not much," he replied. "Coach Green has us practicing hard these days, so I haven't been around much. I haven't gotten much schoolwork done, either."

"I guess none of the players is working too hard in school," Sarah said, thinking of Sky. "Everybody's mind is on winning the championship."

"Yeah," Dave agreed. "But anyone who slips too much is off the team. It's a problem for Sky. I heard that Mrs. Parisi is going to fail him in history."

"Who told you that?" Sarah asked.

"She did," Dave said. "She said that he really messed up his midterm. She told him he could take it again since he's new, but he said he didn't want to do that."

"Why was Mrs. Parisi talking to *you* about Sky?"

"I don't know," Dave said. "Maybe she figured I

was his friend."

"Mrs. Parisi is tough. If you don't pass her tests you don't pass the course," Sarah said. Then she told Dave about what she'd overheard Mr. Cala saying to the coach.

"It sounds like Sky's got more trouble than just Mrs. Parisi," said Dave.

"I guess Coach Green wants all of his teachers to make a pact to pass him, no matter what," said Sarah.

"Well, the real deal is that Mrs. Parisi wants no part of it," Dave said. "And if he fails a couple of courses he could be off the team."

"Ouch! Bad news for Murphy."

"Sarah," Dave said, "what are you doing Saturday night?"

"Saturday night?" Sarah repeated, remembering she had made a date with José. "Umm, I think I'm going to be busy."

"Doing what?" Dave asked.

"Miss Essie asked me to do her hair." Sarah crossed her fingers as she told the lie.

"I don't see much of you anymore," Dave said. "Is something going on with us? I have to make sure I still have my place in your heart. With the whole school going crazy about Sky—you haven't fallen for him, too, have you?"

"Get out of here, man," Sarah said.

"Well, you sure seem to know a lot about him."

Dave's voice had dropped to his intimate tone. "Or are you just interested in the gossip?"

"Just the gossip," Sarah said. An image of José flashed in her mind.

"It had better be the gossip," Dave said.

"And just why are you checking me out?" Sarah asked. "You think you have some competition now and so you're going to finally drop a dime and call the little people?"

"Hey, you don't have to catch an attitude," Dave said.

"Too late!" Sarah said.

"Look, I'm sorry," Dave said. "Can I come over while you're doing Miss Essie's hair?"

"Uh, no." Sarah heard Tasha coming up the stairs. "Look, my mother needs to use the phone. I'll see you in school tomorrow."

"What? Oh, okay," Dave said.

Sarah hung up. Tasha stood there, looking at Sarah. "What was that all about?" she asked.

"Trouble," Sarah said. "Your room or mine?"

"Mine."

They sat down cross-legged on Tasha's bed. "What's happening?" she asked.

"Okay, that was Dave," Sarah explained. "He said he thinks Mrs. Parisi is going to fail Sky in history. He really messed up his midterm."

"I told you I think the dude has trouble reading," Tasha said.

"You think he's illiterate?" Sarah asked.

"No, he just doesn't care," Tasha said. "They call him Sky but they should call him Free Ride. That's what he always thinks he can do, get a free ride because he can play ball."

"That's what Dave called to tell me about," Sarah said.

"I hate to see that kind of thing happen," Tasha said. "My dad used to say he would see guys who were dynamite athletes get themselves messed up with drugs, or not memorizing the plays . . . lame stuff like that."

"And if Mrs. Parisi fails him then all the other teachers will be checking him out," Sarah said.

"What was this bit about your mother wanting to use the phone?" Tasha asked.

"Dave asked me out on Saturday and I have a date with José for that night," Sarah said.

"Careful, cuz," Tasha warned.

"Dave doesn't have a clue about José. He started asking me if I was interested in Sky."

"What?" Tasha asked. "He thought you were going out with Sky? Hope you told him off."

"No, I just played it cool," Sarah said.

"What did he say when you told him you were going out with José?"

"I didn't exactly tell him," Sarah said, embarrassed. "I told him I was going to be doing Miss Essie's hair. Then he wanted to come over anyway and I had to catch an attitude."

"Which one of these guys do you like the best, Sarah?" Tasha asked. "Is it going to be Dave, or is it going to be José?"

"Dave wants it both ways—sometimes he's ready, sometimes he's not," Sarah said. "And José is so sweet. Did you see those flowers and that suit!"

"He's fallen for you, Sarah," Tasha teased.

"I'll have to make up my mind about José," Sarah said. "I guess I've been stringing him along. I like him, but . . . " She shrugged.

"You'll figure it out—or they'll figure it out for you," Tasha said, and changed the subject back to Sky. "Sky really makes me angry," she said. "He's got so much potential, and he's really blowing it, just because he's got an attitude."

"Maybe he's never done well in school. Maybe he's scared."

"You might be right," Tasha said. "If we could show him what it feels like to do well, maybe he'd learn that it's worth some risk to give it a try."

"I don't get it," Sarah said. "A second ago you were going on about how mad Sky made you, and now you're talking about helping him."

"Maybe it's not just Sky's fault. Maybe a system full of people like Coach Green has helped him get by—just because he can play ball." Tasha leaned back against a pillow. "Maybe we can change that a little."

79

"I just thought of something," Sarah said. "Mrs. Parisi's midterm is on African-American history. A lot of our history has been passed on by word of mouth—like the slave narratives and old stories that our great-great-grandparents passed along to our grandparents."

"You mean like the griots, the old storytellers?" Tasha asked.

Sarah nodded. "Yeah, the griots were the ones who kept all the history, all the knowledge of the people. Since most people didn't read or write, they learned their history by listening to them. So if that's how we learned history in the past," she continued, "then why couldn't Mrs. Parisi give Sky an oral exam?"

"The man definitely knows how to talk," Tasha agreed. "But I don't know. I mean, would that be fair? Other kids had to pass the written exam. We're trying to help Sky learn how to succeed, not come up with another way for him to slide by. And how would she even figure out how to grade him?"

"Hey, that's for her to deal with," said Sarah.

"So what do you propose to do?" Tasha asked.

"I don't know." Sarah thought for a moment. "How about starting a petition? We could ask teachers to consider giving oral history exams."

"Maybe you're right. If we can show that the whole school is behind Sky, then maybe Mrs. Parisi will give him another chance," Tasha said. "That boy may be a lost cause, but it won't be because Tasha Gordon didn't give it her best shot."

Sarah had the petition typed by the next morning. It read, "Because African-American culture has a strong oral tradition, students who are required to take history tests having to do with African-Americans should be given the option of taking written or oral tests."

Sarah gave herself the goal of getting at least a hundred signatures on the petition. It was easy to do since Debbie Smith, the leader of Sky's booster squad, was more than willing to help.

Thursday, Sarah made an appointment with Mrs. Parisi to present the petition. They met in the teachers' room. Mrs. Parisi was shorter than Sarah. She had brown shoulder-length hair and hazel eyes, and her skin was the color of Ivory soap. Sarah thought that if she wore funkier clothing, she could pass for a student.

Sarah began her prepared speech. "Mrs. Parisi, over one hundred students at Murphy High have signed this petition—"

"I've heard all about it, Sarah," interrupted the teacher. She took the petition and read it over carefully. "Sit down, Sarah. Let's talk."

"Mrs. Parisi, I really think Sky deserves another chance," Sarah began again. "He's been a victim of a system that wants him to play basketball and do little else—"

"I've offered Sky another chance to study for a real exam," said Mrs. Parisi impatiently, "and so far he has refused my offer. I think there are some things you need to know. First of all, yes, you're right, African-Americans do have a wonderful oral tradition. A lot of American music, literature, and language is based on it. But African-Americans also have a long tradition of the written word in this country. Way back in the eighteenth century, black poets such as Jupiter Hammond, Phillis Wheatley, and George Moses Horton were being published. These were enslaved people, Sarah, who took it upon themselves to learn to read and write, under some very difficult conditions.

"What's more, there was a tradition of literature and of writing in West Africa back in the fifteenth century and in East Africa for hundreds of years before that. What I'm trying to say is that the oral tradition argument just doesn't cut it. And as for Sky, I think I'm being more than fair. In fact, it would be less fair if I allowed Sky to go through my class and passed him simply because he's a good athlete. I have a responsibility to him, Sarah, and I intend to live up to it."

"So that's it—Sky is through?" Sarah said.

Mrs. Parisi shook her head. "No. But if you really want to help your friend Sky, you won't try to make school easier for him. You'll help him understand that school is preparing him for the real world. You'll help him deal with school, instead of the other way around."

Sarah felt embarrassed. She'd been trying to get Sky an easy way out—just the way so many other people in his life had. She wondered whether anyone would have the strength to change Sky's attitude. She took back the petition and stood. Finally she said, "Thank you for your time, Mrs. Parisi."

"I'm glad you came to speak with me," the teacher said. "I also have something for you."

"What's this?" Sarah asked, taking the paper Mrs. Parisi handed her.

"A list of books that will tell you something about the intellectual accomplishments of Africans and African-Americans."

Tasha was waiting anxiously for Sarah outside the teachers' room. "So, how did it go? Is she going to give him the oral exam?"

"No," said Sarah.

"Why not? Didn't she understand?" asked Tasha.

"Yes, she understood." Sarah waved the list of African-American achievements at Tasha. "It's just that she thinks the African-American tradition of writing is just as strong."

"So what's next?" Tasha asked.

"If Sky Hodges is going to pass history and play basketball for Murphy, he has to pass that exam. And if Sky is going to pass her course, he's going to have to do it the same way everybody else does." Sarah sighed.

"Well, we tried, didn't we, cousin?"

"No, Tasha, we didn't try the right thing," Sarah said. "We tried to do what everyone else has tried to do for Sky—sneak him through. If we really want to do something for him, we've got to help him pass this exam."

"Hey, girl, you sure do like a challenge, don't you," Tasha said as they walked down the hall. She paused. "You know, my father always told me to do the right thing—no matter how hard it was. Sky may be a little bit of a jerk, but if we don't help him now, he'll probably never get it. Okay, I'm in. Where do we start?"

Sarah smiled and told Tasha her plan.

When the doorbell rang on Saturday evening, Sarah checked herself out in the hallway mirror one last time before opening the door for José. She liked the way her new waves framed her face and set off her smile, and the way the pearls Miss Essie had lent her looked on her soft peach blouse. José stopped in the doorway and inhaled sharply when he saw her.

Sarah smiled. "It's okay, José. You can breathe now." She called good night to her parents and they left.

José said very little on the way downtown. Sarah wondered if he was upset by how little they'd seen each other over the past week. Sarah had been so busy she'd hardly been to 18 Pine. He finally spoke in the restaurant.

"Sarah, I hope you don't mind that I've been staring at you," he said. "You are just so beautiful."

Sarah smiled uncomfortably. "You look nice, too," she said. "I really like your suit. Blue looks great on you." The glow of the candlelight on José's dark hair added to the romance of the moment.

"It's different from the sweatshirt-and-jeans look at school, right?" José said.

"That's all right for school," Sarah said. "It's fun to dress up sometimes, though."

"It's a good thing you don't dress like this in school," José went on. "No one could study anything except you."

"Maybe we should look at the menu," Sarah said.

She was glad to be at a restaurant where the menu was more interesting than the pizza toppings at 18 Pine St. "The pasta is supposed to be really good here," she told José. "I think I'll have a salad, fettuccine Alfredo, and an iced tea."

"Hmm, I guess I'll have the spiciest thing on the menu—the spaghetti and peppers," said José.

The waiter took their order. José continued to stare at Sarah. She had to admit that she liked the attention.

"Sarah, what's going on with you and Dave?" he asked.

Sarah tensed. "We're just good friends," she answered. She folded her hands on the table.

"Good friends like you and I are good friends?" José asked.

Sarah laughed. "José, come on. You're not jealous, are you? After all, we're not going steady."

"No. I just think you're so terrific—and I don't want to share" he answered.

"Actually," she said, remembering the phone conversation she'd had with Dave the other night, "Dave and I hardly speak to each other."

"Really?" José said. "I thought there was still something between the two of you."

"Not anymore," Sarah replied, trying not to sound sad. She looked down. This was getting uncomfortable. She decided to change the subject. "What's your family like, José?" she asked.

"I've got seven brothers and sisters, so the place is always loud," he said. "As I was telling your mom at dinner last week, my mom's a surgeon, and my dad is a writer. He works for *Undercover* magazine. They're really great—for parents." He covered her hands with his.

Sarah felt as if her hands were melting.

"Tell me, you like to dance to salsa?" José asked. There was gentle pressure on Sarah's hands.

"I like to dance to anything, really," Sarah said. "And you?"

"I like it better than hip-hop for dancing. My

cousin Manny is going to have a party next month. He might even have a live band. Maybe you can go with me—"

"I'd love to," Sarah heard herself saying before she even thought about what she would be doing next month.

"Somehow I knew you would like to dance," José said. "When I think of you I think of movement, of gentle rhythms and big moons. I could teach you to speak to the moon in Spanish."

"Why . . . why would I want to speak to the moon?" Sarah asked.

"Because only the moon knows all the secrets of love," José said. "And, of course, the moon only speaks Spanish."

"Very convenient since *you* speak Spanish," Sarah said.

As they left the restaurant, José put his arm around Sarah's waist. Sarah had to admit to herself that she'd had a great time. The food had been fabulous and José had made her laugh with his stories about his seven brothers and sisters. In the taxi on the way home, she rested her head on his shoulder. At her door, they kissed good night.

Finally he said quietly, "I enjoyed being with you tonight. Tomorrow I have relatives over all day. Why don't you come over for dinner?"

Sarah hesitated. "Hey, I came to your house,"

José reminded her.

Sarah nodded and said, "Sure," and he lightly kissed her forehead and turned away to go home.

When she was lying in bed later that night, she replayed the candlelight dinner and José's gentle good-night kiss in her mind. There was no denying that it had been a wonderful evening. José was a dream come true—good-looking, smart, romantic. When she was with him she felt alive and beautiful. Yet something was holding her back.

Sarah felt a knot form in her stomach. She didn't understand how someone could make her so happy and so uncomfortable at the same time. She hoped she'd find out soon.

Nine

Sarah called Jennifer first thing Sunday morning and woke her up. "If you really want to help Sky, meet Tasha and me at the library at ten."

"Whoa." Jennifer was still groggy. "What's this about?"

"Mrs. Parisi said she would give Sky another chance at the history exam. But she's not giving him much time, so he's got to study for it or he's just going to flunk it again."

"So why don't you just ask him if he wants to study for it?" Jennifer asked.

"I mentioned it on Friday and he just gave me this big grin and shook his head like I was something stupid," Sarah said.

"Oh," Jennifer replied. "Why do we have to

meet at the library?"

"We're meeting there because if Sky comes bopping into 18 Pine you know there's going to be a crowd around him and nobody's going to get serious. You've got to talk to him, Jennifer," Sarah continued. "I mean, if you think that succeeding in one class can help get him on track."

Sarah waited for Jennifer to say something. Instead she heard quiet sobs. Sarah wondered if Jennifer and Sky had fallen out.

"You okay?" she asked.

"Look." Jennifer was crying. "I know Sky has trouble with his schoolwork. We were at the mall and there were some signs he couldn't read. I kind of mentioned it to him, and he acted as if I was dissing him or something. He told me he didn't have any use for la-de-da chicks."

"La-de-da?" Sarah said. "What did he mean by that?"

"He means girls who think they're special and need their men to speak properly, and do well in school and stuff. He says I'm trying to be white."

"You're trying to be *what*?" Sarah was getting mad. She caught herself. "No, that's just his cover. He doesn't want to admit that he's got a problem. So when you mentioned it to him he tried to turn it back on you. No, a lot of people who have trouble reading try to cover it up. Miss Essie told me about a friend of hers who used to say that her eyes were bad and

90

would have people read things to her."

"And she really couldn't read herself?" Jennifer asked. She had stopped crying.

"Nope," Sarah said. "But nobody knew it for a long time. You know, it's probably embarrassing for Sky not to do well in school. Especially when he does so well playing basketball."

"Okay, I'll see you at the library. And Sky will be there," Jennifer said.

At the library, Tasha, Jennifer, and Sarah staked out a table in the corner. Sky headed toward them, stopping for a moment to look at the video rack.

"If I was getting up a fan club," Sky said, "I'd start with you three right here."

"Hi, baby." Jennifer smiled at him.

"So what's this big meeting about?" Sky asked, checking his watch. "I'm kind of pressed for time."

"Sky." Jennifer took a deep breath. "The word around the school is that if you don't do better in your classes you're going to be dropped from the team."

"The coach didn't tell me that," Sky said. "You running the team now?"

"Lighten up, Sky," Tasha said. "Jennifer's trying to give you the word. If you keep failing your tests you will be off the team, that's a school policy."

"Jennifer, Tasha, and I are offering our help. Mrs. Parisi is willing to give you a makeup test on African-

American history, and we're willing to tutor you," said Sarah.

Sky folded his arms. "So tell me what I'm supposed to know," he said. Sarah rolled her eyes and looked at Jennifer.

"For starters," Jennifer explained, "you need to know that the Harlem Renaissance has to do with the great flowering of African-American culture between World War One and Two."

Sky smiled and put his arm around her shoulders. Jennifer pulled away. "Listen, Sky, this is serious. Mrs. Parisi is giving you a special makeup test. We want to help you pass it. We want you to know what it's like to pass a test on your own, without help from basketball."

"Sky, let's check something out," Sarah said. "What do you know about African-American history?"

Sky shrugged. "Like what?"

"Like who was called 'The Father of Black History' and what did he do?" Sarah asked.

"Why don't you just tell me?"

"Because you're supposed to know this stuff," said Sarah, exasperated.

"It was Carter G. Woodson," Jennifer said. "He started the first Negro History Week in 1926 and now it's grown into African-American History Month."

"And what about Zora Neale Hurston?" asked Sarah.

92

"I must have been out when they taught that," Sky said.

"She wrote one of my favorite books, *Their Eyes Were Watching God*," Jennifer said.

Sky grinned at Jennifer. "Well, baby, if you like it, maybe I should take a look at it."

"Maybe you should try actually reading it," said Sarah. "Look, Sky, I think that you're dissing all this schoolwork because you're afraid of it. We can help you see that you *can* do the work. But we can't help you unless you want us to."

Sky stood up. "I gotta get moving. I've got some business that needs taking care of."

"Wait, Sky," Jennifer pleaded. "The makeup test is tomorrow."

"Let him go, Jennifer," Tasha said. "It's pretty obvious that he doesn't want our help."

Sky laughed. "It's you ladies who'll be needing my help someday. And just remember—when you need something from me, hey, the Sky's the limit."

The three girls watched as Sky made his way to the exit.

PINE

Ten

By Sunday afternoon, Sarah was nervous. Meeting José's family had seemed like fun the first time he mentioned it, but now she realized how afraid she was. She kept telling herself that his family would be nice and would like her, but she knew she wasn't sure. It seemed silly, but she had never been to a Hispanic family's house and didn't know what to expect.

José's house was in an older section of Madison, where the houses were very expensive and the gardens were quite beautiful.

"Look for the house number," Mrs. Gordon said as she slowed the Volvo.

Sarah wasn't sure what she had been expecting, but she was surprised when number 114 turned out to be a split-level house with red trim and a beautiful red-brick driveway.

"Have fun," Mrs. Gordon called out as Sarah stepped from the car. "Call me if you need a ride home."

Sarah waved as Mrs. Gordon drove off. Then she looked back at José's house. A curtain opened and shut quickly in an upstairs window. Sarah went to the front door, hesitated a minute as the brightly colored wind chimes seemed to announce her presence, and then rang the bell.

"Hey, you made it," José said as he opened the door. He gave Sarah a quick kiss on the cheek and stepped aside for her to enter.

Sarah stepped into a small hallway. She could hear soft rock music coming from the basement. A short flight of steps led up to the living room. Two young girls and a boy waved at Sarah over the back of a white couch. Sarah smiled and waved back and the little children giggled.

"Off the couch! Off the couch!" The woman striding into the room spoke without looking at the children.

"Sarah, this is my mother," José said.

"Sarah, do yourself a big favor," Mrs. Melendez said. "Don't have children!"

"You're lucky," José said to Sarah. "All of my cousins have gone home—or else there would be ten more here for dinner."

Sarah laughed and followed José into the kitchen after his mother.

"Every Sunday I cook food his father thinks is Puerto Rican," Mrs. Melendez joked. "Only he left Puerto Rico when he was four and he doesn't know a thing about the island."

Sarah watched as Mrs. Melendez carefully put sliced plantains into a pan of diced onions. She added some spices that Sarah had never smelled before.

"Excellent fiber," Mrs. Melendez said.

"That's the doctor in her coming out," José said.

"*¿Oye, no me vas a presentar, niño?*"

Sarah was startled at the sound of an elderly person's voice. She turned and saw a woman in the doorway. She had dark hair streaked with gray that came down to her shoulders. On her dress she wore a pearl pendant whose black, smoky lines complemented her hair.

"This is my great-grandmother," said José. "We call her *Abuela*; it means grandmother. She won't stand for great-grandmother." José rattled off a string of Spanish words and Sarah caught her name. The old woman smiled and bowed her head in greeting. Sarah smiled back.

Next José's two brothers came in. One was tall and thin, and the other one was shorter with dimples.

"My dad's going to come in next," José said. "Count on it."

Almost before he could get the words out, a tall, handsome man walked in. "José, are you going to introduce me to your friend?"

"Sarah, this is my father." José bowed slightly from the waist.

"My pleasure," Sarah said, smiling,

"I'm glad to see that my son has finally trapped a girl into coming home with him," Mr. Melendez said.

"Dad!"

Sarah's stomach suddenly started to feel queasy. The smell of cooking oil, spices, and garlic was overwhelming. She glanced at her watch: 6:15. She felt guilty about wanting to leave, but all the strange faces and the fast clatter of Spanish were almost too much for her.

"Out of my kitchen!" José's mother waved them off and the Melendez family instantly scattered. Sarah thought it wasn't too much different from her own home.

During dinner José's brothers Arturo and Joaquin shot questions at her. Mostly they were silly questions, trying to find out if José really had a girl-friend—Allison would have loved the scene. Sarah answered them politely until they lost interest and spoke among themselves in Spanish. Every time she glanced at Abuela, the old woman was looking at her.

Even José forgot himself a few times and started

98

speaking in Spanish until Sarah nudged him. This must be what it's like to be an exchange student in a foreign country, she thought.

"I have to apologize for all the Spanish being spoken at the dinner table," Mr. Melendez said. "It's very difficult to maintain our own Hispanic cultural heritage as well as our American heritage, so I insist that we speak Spanish at dinner."

"That's really cool—I mean exciting," Sarah said.

"I think it's pretty cool, too," Mr. Melendez said. "Word down! Is that the expression?"

"Maybe 'word up,' Sarah said, "but you're close enough."

The rest of the meal went pleasantly. Sarah liked being the center of attention, and she realized that José must have been telling his family a lot about her. The food was odd. She had eaten plantains, which tasted like bananas but not as sweet, at Cindy's house, but Mrs. Melendez cooked them differently. The chicken with rice was a bit like the kind her mom made, but it tasted a little funny.

Sarah asked about Mrs. Melendez's work at the hospital, but José's mother just shrugged the question off.

"José said that you save a lot of lives," Sarah said.

"It's good to save lives," Mrs. Melendez answered. "But it's bad that there are so many lives that need saving."

After they had finished dinner, José took her to

the bedroom he shared with one of his brothers to work on their math homework.

"So what do you think of my family?" he asked, eagerly.

"Your mom must be a Superwoman," Sarah said. She got up from her chair to close the bedroom door, but José stopped her.

"Leave it open," he said quickly. "It wouldn't look right."

"We're not going to do anything," said Sarah. She looked out into the hallway and saw Joaquin walk into the bathroom. "I just wanted some privacy."

"We've got privacy," José insisted. "It's just . . . my family is a little old-fashioned. It doesn't look right for me to have the door closed with a girl in here."

Don't they trust us? Sarah was about to say. Instead she kept quiet. She went back to her chair and opened José's math book. If that's the way things were in José's family, who was she to argue?

"But anyway," José said. "You do like my family, right?"

"José, they're so nice," Sarah said. "They're so warm."

"Warm and nosy," José said, smiling. He had a wide mouth and even white teeth. "They see everybody as a potential family member."

They worked on José's trigonometry until it was time for Sarah to leave. José's father drove them to the Gordons' home.

"I feel like I'm being racist because I didn't enjoy myself as much as José wanted me to," Sarah admitted to her mother as they stood in the kitchen.

"Because you didn't like the food and couldn't understand the language?" Mrs. Gordon asked.

Sarah nodded.

"I was so nervous," she said. "I kept thinking that I would mess things up because I didn't know Spanish or because I would do something to upset them. You know what I mean?"

"Different is good if your mind is open," Mrs. Gordon said. "Sometimes it's hard to open your mind because you're too worried about what kind of impression you're making, and sometimes a different culture takes time to get used to. The food and the language are part of what makes them Puerto Rican."

"Not to mention the loud music, and the kids running around," said Sarah with a laugh.

Mrs. Gordon didn't respond. After a few seconds, she said, "Well, now you *are* being racist. Being an active family has nothing to do with being Puerto Rican. A family with a few kids is going to be noisy, even if they're from Nebraska. You'd have to get used to that no matter where José came from."

"I know," Sarah said quietly. "I'm just not sure how I feel about José." Why did she keep changing her mind about him? she wondered. She couldn't wait to go upstairs to her familiar room and lie on her familiar bed. And close the door all the way if I want to, she thought ruefully.

Eleven

The next day Sarah saw Kwame in study hall. "Sarah, you deserve the golden heart medal. I don't know why you bother. The brother just doesn't get it."

"I take it you're talking about Sky. Did he show up for his test?" she asked.

"He showed up. Got to give him that," he said.

"Don't tell me he blew it?"

Kwame shrugged. "I really can't tell. All I know is that Mrs. Parisi came into Mr. Miller's office and showed him the test paper. When they saw me they stopped talking. But I did hear her say, 'I gave him an essay test so that he could have the chance to develop his own ideas and this is what I got.' When Mr. Miller looked at the paper, he sat down and

103

shook his head. I tell you, Sarah, from where I was, I didn't notice much writing on the paper."

"Kwame, you actually sound concerned," said Sarah.

"In a way I am. Underneath all those gold chains Sky is a talented guy who just doesn't have his priorities straight. When you see him play basketball, you know he's not dumb. He just needs some help."

Sarah nodded. "Well, one thing's for sure—he doesn't want my help."

"He doesn't want anyone's help," Kwame said. "The way I see it, it's sort of like my practicing really hard so I can make the basketball team."

"You?" Sarah smiled. "What do you mean, Kwame? I've seen you play."

"My point exactly," Kwame said. "For me, there's no point in working at playing ball—I'll never make the team anyway. I think that's how Sky feels about hitting the books. He doesn't think he's going to make the grade." He paused. "But the difference is, basketball is just a sport. A few people make a living at it, but for most people, it's just a game. Reading and writing pay off in the long run."

"That's good thinking, Kwame," Sarah said. "Maybe Sky would listen to you. Why don't you talk to him?"

Kwame shook his head. "He has to want to help himself, and I don't think Sky's there yet. Besides that, I have my own tests to worry about."

"Oh, Kwame, you're one of those guys who just has to show up in class and eat the right kind of pepperoni pizza and you get an A," said Sarah.

"Pepperoni pizza may be my secret weapon, but it's not the only one. Why do you think I'm here in study hall every day with these books open?" he asked.

"Because this is when the girls' pep club has study hall." Sarah poked him in the ribs with her elbow.

"Oh, yeah, they're over there? I didn't even notice them." Kwame gave her a big smile.

"Hey Dave!" Sky called when Dave Hunter entered 18 Pine St. Sarah looked up anxiously. The last thing she wanted was for Dave to join everyone at the table. José had told her that he might stop by 18 Pine just to see her. She wasn't clear on her feelings about Dave, and she certainly was confused about José. Dealing with both at the same time would be too much.

To Sarah's relief, Sky got up and ushered Dave over to another table. The two of them sat huddled together for a few minutes. Then Dave waved for her to come over. What does he want? Sarah wondered as she joined them. She hadn't spoken to Dave since she'd lied to him about her date on the phone that night.

Sky spoke to both of them. "Man, what is wrong

with this Parisi woman?"

"What do you mean?" Sarah asked.

"I couldn't do a thing on that special test she gave me."

"You mean you failed?" Sarah asked.

"You got that right," Sky said. "And she's being real hard-nosed about it. She says she's already given me a second chance. When she asked me what I expected her to do, I told her to pass me, of course. I've already made the effort by taking this second test, now it's up to her, man."

"What did she say?" asked Dave.

"Nothing. I think she expected me to fall down and start begging or something," Sky said. "And you know that begging is not my thing."

"She could make a real problem for you on the team," said Dave.

"Yeah, man, I know. And that's why I'm talking to you. You two are definitely her favorite types."

"I've already gone to bat for you, Sky." Sarah wasn't smiling. "I got embarrassed in front of one of my favorite teachers."

"How about you, Dave? Doesn't Parisi like you?" Sky asked.

"I guess so. I've always liked history, so I did okay in her class," said Dave.

"Yeah, man, so why don't you drop by her class and talk to her?" Sky said.

"What do you expect me to say?" asked Dave.

"Should I say, 'Look, Sky is a great ballplayer and you ought to pass him because he's too lazy to study?'" Dave paused. "You're a key member of the team, man, but you got to make it easier to help you."

"You want me on the team, you figure it out. Tell her how I fit in with the team and how the school is behind me and everything," Sky said. "You know, she'll be going against the whole school."

"Yeah, okay." Dave looked away from Sarah. Sarah realized Dave was as frustrated with Sky as everyone else was.

"I knew you were my man," Sky said as he stood up. Dave nodded reluctantly and they gave each other high fives. Sky left Sarah with Dave.

"I'm going over to sit with the others," said Sarah. Dave didn't seem to want to talk with her about the date on Saturday, and she was willing to let the tension stand.

She didn't feel good about what Dave had agreed to do for Sky. She didn't think Dave felt good about it, either.

Twelve

"Look at this, Sarah," said Tasha, pointing to the sports page on Tuesday morning.

"Tasha, give me a break," Sarah groaned. "Let me have my orange juice first."

"Yeah, but it's about Sky," said Allison, who was busy stuffing her face with syrupy waffles.

"What about him?" Sarah looked over Tasha's shoulder.

"This is an article about Sky's problems at school. Someone at school must have called the reporter and told him about the hassles Sky's been having with his classes. The article isn't just about Sky's problems at Murphy. The reporter also spoke to Sky's old coach at Countee Cullen High School in Baltimore," explained Tasha. She poured more granola and milk into her bowl.

"Where's Dad?" Sarah asked. She got a muffin and orange juice for her breakfast and sat at the table.

Tasha said, "He's in his study. He was really angry when he saw the article."

"Why is Dad so interested in Sky? Dad is principal at Hamilton High, not Murphy," Sarah said.

"It's about students, I think," Tasha said. "I guess it's part of being a principal. Here he comes now."

Mr. Gordon walked into the kitchen. He poured himself a cup of coffee and sat at the table. "I got a call from one of Sky's old teachers yesterday," he said. "He teaches French at Countee Cullen and doubles as guidance counselor. He and I went to Howard together."

"He was Sky's counselor?" Tasha asked.

"Yes. He told me a reporter called him last week. At first he was asked some questions about how Sky got his start, how he developed into such a fine athlete and things like that." Mr. Gordon took a sip of coffee. "Then, just when he thought the interview was over, the reporter came on strong with questions about Sky's academic standing at Countee Cullen."

"Did Sky have the same kinds of problems at Cullen as he does at Murphy?" asked Sarah.

Mr. Gordon looked at his daughter. "Sarah, I get so angry about what happens to athletes like Sky, sometimes it's hard to talk about it."

Sarah was puzzled. "But Daddy, you don't even know Sky. Why are you so upset?"

"I don't personally know Sky. But I certainly know of him and lots of other athletes like him. And I don't like what I see," he answered.

"What do you mean?" asked Tasha.

"My friend told me that Sky had transferred to Countee Cullen about two years ago in the middle of the school year. It seems that his previous school, Martin Luther King High, had asked for the transfer because Sky couldn't keep up his grades."

"What was the point of just sending him to another school?" Sarah asked. "He'd have to keep up his grades wherever he went."

"But as long as people are willing to see Sky as just a good ballplayer, instead of as a student—and there are lots of people out there like that—he can continue to fool himself into thinking that everything is going to be all right," Mr. Gordon said. "He figures that any college will jump at the chance to have him—even if his grades stink."

"People are helping him fool himself because they want his basketball talents," Sarah said.

Mr. Gordon nodded. "The reporter found out that Sky had mostly passing grades at Countee Cullen," he continued, "so he asked if they were just passing Sky to let him play ball."

"Were they?" Tasha asked. She glanced at Sarah. They were both thinking about the conversation

111

between Coach Green and Mr. Cala that Sarah had overheard.

"Probably. But my friend couldn't actually say that they did. But you see, this is what makes me so angry. These schools love to have winning teams. And in order to have them, they have to have athletes who can play well. Well, you cannot be a good student if the coach has you in practice all day. So these guys get transferred out of school after school because they can't do the academic work, and the coaches, the very ones who kept them out of classes, worry that their teams will be disqualified on academic grounds."

"You know, I can see how it happens," Tasha said. "If a guy can play basketball, he can convince himself that it's the only way he can make it in life. My father used to say that he was born with a gift, and that he had to use his gift one hundred percent."

"Tasha, your father had problems like this, too," Mr. Gordon said.

"My father wasn't anything like Sky," snapped Tasha. She looked upset.

"No, not exactly," Mr. Gordon said gently. "From what I hear about Sky, I'd say that your father was much more modest about his talent. He was a great football player, so the coaches always wanted to take advantage of that. He had a problem with his grades because he never had enough time to study. After he was transferred to another high school, I helped him as much as I could with his assignments. I was very proud of him when he went to college."

"You tutored him the way we're trying to do with Sky?" asked Sarah.

"Yes. I was a few years older than he was so I knew most of the subjects he was taking. Actually, he was a smart guy. Sometimes, when he took the time to study, he knew the work better than I did." Mr. Gordon smiled.

"So the tutoring helped?" asked Tasha.

"Absolutely. Eventually he learned how to get the important things in order. He wanted to make a career of football and he knew that he had to go to college to get on a pro team. So he had no choice. He had to learn how to make time for his schoolwork," Mr. Gordon said.

"How can we help Sky to see that?" asked Sarah.

"It's hard," said Mr. Gordon, "because guys like Sky have a lot of hard work to do just to catch up, and they usually don't want to do the work."

"Sky doesn't seem to understand what's happening to him," said Tasha.

"Neither did your father at first," said Mr. Gordon. "He was so caught up in the glamour of being a star. It's hard to keep your head straight when people are telling you how great you are."

"I didn't know all this about my father," said Tasha. "I guess things turned out fine for him. I'm not sure we'll be able to say the same thing about Sky."

PINE

Thirteen

"Tasha, are you okay?" Sarah poked her head into Tasha's bedroom.

"I'm fine, I guess," Tasha said. She was sitting on her bed with her guitar on her lap. "I was just thinking about what your father said."

"It sounds like your father was really lucky to have people around who cared enough to help him," Sarah said.

Tasha leaned back on her pillows. "I think we have to try harder with Sky so that he doesn't get into this mess that your father was talking about."

"Sky's already in it. He doesn't want to do the work," Sarah said. She told Tasha about Sky's asking Dave to talk to Mrs. Parisi.

Tasha shook her head. "The guy's lazy—there's

115

no doubt about it. Lazy or scared, anyway. I guess I'm just not ready to believe that Sky is a lost cause."

"Jennifer called before. Do you think if we organize a different sort of tutoring session for Sky he'll be more interested?" Sarah asked.

"I don't know. Jennifer really wants to help, but I don't think it will work," Tasha said. "Sky might ignore it just because it has to do with school. But if she wants to do it, and if he goes along, I'm willing to help."

"Any ideas on how we can do it? I think we need to be less threatening," Sarah said.

Tasha thought about it for a while. "Okay, here's the deal. Steve and Kwame are good at math. April gets good marks in English. Cindy and Dave are best at history. Jennifer is good at—"

"—Moral support," interrupted Sarah.

"Uh-huh, sure. And you and I are just natural geniuses all around."

"True, true," Sarah agreed.

"So there's our group. Let's call a meeting of tutors for Monday afternoon at 18 Pine St. We'll serve pizza and run it like a quiz show. That way Sky won't feel like he's studying."

"Jennifer will like your plan," Sarah said, "but haven't you forgotten something? How do we get Sky there?"

"Easy. We tell Jennifer to bring him," said Tasha.

116

*   *   *

The scene at their table at 18 Pine St. was different from most other days after school. All the tutors were there with books piled high in front of them. There wasn't much room left for the two pizzas they had ordered. Kwame had even brought a plastic microphone so he could act as emcee for the game show. The big question was—where were Sky and Jennifer?

Cindy turned to Tasha. "Are you sure you told Jennifer to be here at four?"

"Why should you expect him to show up?" Kwame asked.

"Kwame," said Steve, "you said you'd try to be more open-minded about this."

"Yeah, that's right. I came here to help, didn't I?" said Kwame.

April was looking at a thick American literature textbook. "I think you guys gave me the biggest job. How can I tutor him on these stories if he has trouble reading?"

"Maybe, then, you should just help him read," Cindy said.

"I dug up my notes from Mrs. Parisi's history class." Dave put two spiral bound notebooks on top of his other books. "I think I should have the most time with him, since he's having the most trouble with her."

"Well, there's the man himself." Kwame was

looking up at the door.

Sky's swagger was even more pronounced than usual. He raised his eyebrows and smirked when he saw the pile of books in front of the group at the table. Jennifer was holding his arm.

"Attitude!" Kwame muttered.

"Well, look at all these folks just waiting to see me," Sky said to Jennifer.

Sarah braced herself. This was going to be even harder than she thought.

"Look, man," Dave said, keeping his voice even, "we're all here because we want to help you with your grades."

"We can tutor you in all of your subjects," Tasha explained. "We've set up a system for doing this. All you have to do is tell us when you'd like to do it."

"What am I going to be, your class project or something?" Sky asked. "I don't dig all this rah-rah stuff. You know, you people are on a dream kick. It's running into my reality and I don't like it."

"And what is your reality, man?" Tasha asked.

"My reality is that I've got a chance to make it big, and I'm going for it," Sky said. "You people are grinding away so that you can be some nine-to-five slaves who have a couple of credit cards. I'm not about what you people are about. I'm looking for the top. You know, the cars, the money, the headlines, the women. I want the whole trip."

"Without some kind of grades, Sky . . . " Jennifer

didn't finish her sentence.

"We're wasting our time, people," said Kwame.

Sky leaned back in his chair and grinned at Kwame. "You're wasting your life, Mr. Brown."

Kwame's lips tightened, but he didn't say anything.

Sarah flinched. This was not the way this meeting was supposed to go.

"Look, Sky," said Steve. "We all think you've been great for Murphy and we want to do something for you."

"Well, now you're talking," said Sky. "For all I've done to put Murphy on the map, you're *supposed* to help me. I mean, where would your pitiful little basketball team be without me?"

"It's a team sport!" Dave said from across the table. "And if you're not making progress in school by the big Watertown game, Coach Green might not even let you play."

"I don't mean you. You're okay, man. Without us there wouldn't be a team. That's what I mean," said Sky.

Kwame had heard enough. He stood up. "Well, I don't know what you mean. But whatever it is, I don't want anything to do with it. I've got my own tests to pass. And as for the team, I don't really care about it one way or another. I'll get into college without it. And you, the way you're going—talented or not—you won't make it into college to play bas-

119

ketball. You can't even stay in high school. You'd better check yourself out, man."

Kwame picked up his books and started to walk away from the table.

Sky stood up. "Hold on, Kwame." Kwame stood still. "Let's say that all that stuff about you is right. But what you said about me, man, you just don't get it. I hear you are a good student. You study a lot. Well, I practice a lot and I'm a good basketball player. So, that's where that's at, man. *You* check it out."

"Sky, I did that already. So now I'm checking out. I'll catch you folks later." Kwame waved at them and left the pizzeria.

April stood up next. "You know," she said, "I'm not so sure that I'm going to really be able to do this tutoring. I have to—"

"It's okay, April," said Sarah. "It doesn't look like anyone will be tutoring Sky. He doesn't want the help."

Tasha gave Sky a list of the tutors' phone numbers and subjects. "Here. Call us when you're ready to deal with the real world."

Fourteen

The game against Watertown was the biggest one of the season. If Murphy won they'd have an automatic invitation to the state tournament. The word was out that Sky might be dropped from the team. Tasha, Sarah, and April sat together near half-court.

"So, I guess he's going to play," April said. "He's warming up."

"He'll still be on the team," Sarah said. "But he won't play unless all of his teachers give the okay."

"All of them?" April asked. "Why not just a majority?"

"I think because of the article in the paper," Sarah answered. "You want to get some potato chips?"

"No, I'm off junk food," April said. "And anyway, I've already had two bags."

"Whoa! How can you be off junk food and have two bags of potato chips?" Tasha said.

"That was supper," April said. "My dad's out of town and my stepmom left a frozen dinner on top of the microwave. Now that's really junk food."

"Here comes Mrs. Parisi," Sarah said. "She's headed right for us."

"Hi, girls." Mrs. Parisi had her hands in the pocket of her long corduroy skirt. She was wearing a belt with a handmade Indian buckle. "Mind if I join you?"

"Sure," Tasha said. "I didn't know you liked basketball."

"I don't, particularly," Mrs. Parisi answered. "It's a big game, though, and everyone at Murphy will be talking about it all day tomorrow—so I thought I'd come see for myself."

"Do you think Sky will be playing?" April asked. "I heard that Mr. Cala said he could play."

"All the teachers except one approved Sky's playing tonight," she said. "And I'm the one. I thought I might as well come here and take my lumps."

"Hey . . . " Sarah wanted to say something that would make it seem all right, but she couldn't think of a thing.

Sky was sitting on the bench as the teams lined up for the start of the game. Watertown got the ball first and their center missed an easy basket. Dave got the rebound and Murphy brought the ball downcourt

122

quickly. Billy drove down one side of the lane and threw an alley-oop for Dave. Dave caught the ball high in the air and slammed it down.

Sarah jumped up and started cheering. Despite the tension between her and Dave, she still wanted him to succeed.

Murphy scored the next six points, and they were up 8 to 0.

"Yes! Yes!" April was getting excited and banging Tasha on the arm.

The Watertown players seemed tentative at first, and then began to relax. They switched from a man-to-man defense to a tight zone. They were boxing Dave in whenever they could.

Murphy turned the ball over twice and soon the score was 8 to 4. A minute later, the game was tied.

"Get the ball to Dave!" somebody shouted.

"They're trying, you idiot!" somebody else shouted back.

By halftime the score was 32 to 20, in Watertown's favor.

"We'll do better in the second half," Tasha said positively. "The coach will come up with something."

"I hope so," Mrs. Parisi said.

By two minutes into the second half, it was clear that the coach hadn't come up with anything. Watertown was leading 40 to 22.

"Sky! Sky! Sky!"

The Murphy High crowd chanted Sky's name. Tasha took a quick look at Mrs. Parisi. She looked very uncomfortable.

"My dad was a professional football player," Tasha said to the teacher.

"I've heard," said Mrs. Parisi. "Mr. Cala told me."

Tasha cringed at the sound of Mr. Cala's name, but continued, "He made something of his career, and I think he was glad that he pursued it. But my uncle told me that my father worked hard to get through school, and managed to get more than sports training. I think part of that learning came from teachers who had the guts to follow through, teachers like you."

Mrs. Parisi looked straight at Tasha. She paused for a second, then said softly, "Thanks, Tasha."

The crowd at 18 Pine St. was unusually quiet.

"We got all the way to the end of the season and this had to happen." Dave shook his head. Sarah couldn't remember ever seeing him this upset.

"Hey, Dave," she said softly, "this was your best game of the season, I think."

Sky nodded. "Sarah's right, man. You were the star of both teams."

"It was because of Mrs. Parisi that we lost," said Jennifer bitterly. "Is that what she was talking to you about during the game—how great it felt to see Murphy lose?"

"Actually," Tasha said, "she was hoping that Murphy would win, just like everybody else."

"Well, there's no reason to blame anyone," Sarah said.

"Oh, yeah. Right." Sky seemed to lose interest in the conversation. He hung his head and started to eat his cold pizza.

The next day when Sarah and Allison arrived home after picking up some dessert for Mrs. Gordon from the bakery, they heard the soft strumming of Tasha's guitar coming from the living room. Sarah looked in to see Miss Essie and an elderly gentleman sitting on the couch. Miss Essie put her finger on her lips. Sarah put down the box of walnut brownies and listened as Tasha finished playing.

Tasha ended the piece with a soft arpeggio, then bowed ever so slightly.

"Bravo!" The gentleman sitting with Miss Essie stood and applauded. He was about Miss Essie's age and fairly handsome, though not as dapper as Mr. Taylor.

"Sarah and Allison, this is Mr. Houston," Miss Essie said. "We've known each other for many years."

Mr. Houston smiled and shook Sarah's, then Allison's hand. He did not say anything.

"Ben is the quiet type," Miss Essie said.

"Tasha, you play beautifully," he said.

"I haven't heard that piece, have I?" Sarah asked.

"It's an old song that I used to play a lot," Tasha said.

"What's everyone waiting for?" Sarah asked.

"Miss Essie is waiting for your mom and dad," Tasha said.

"And I'm looking forward to seeing Donald's face when we tell him the news!" Miss Essie said.

"So is somebody going to tell me or what?" Allison asked as they heard the front door being unlocked.

Mr. and Mrs. Gordon came in together. They had gone grocery shopping after work. Mr. Gordon was carrying four shopping bags, one of which looked as if it was going to fall at any second. Sarah ran to help him with it. When he saw Miss Essie and her friend, Mr. Gordon smiled and said hello.

"We'll be right back," Mrs. Gordon said as they both went into the kitchen.

"Sit down, Ben, and relax," Miss Essie said. Meanwhile, she was anxiously pacing the floor.

"Miss Essie," Sarah said, "why don't *you* sit down?"

When Mr. and Mrs. Gordon came into the living room, Miss Essie and Mr. Houston were sitting on the sofa. Miss Essie stood up. "Donald and Elizabeth, this is Ben Houston," she said. "We have an announcement."

Mr. Gordon groaned. "Shall I sit down for this

one? Another marriage proposal?"

Miss Essie laughed. "Not this time," she said, blushing. "Ben is an old friend, from . . . a long time ago," she continued. "He used to be a detective, and when I called him and told him I needed a little help, he came out of retirement for me."

Mr. Houston smiled.

Miss Essie continued, "I told Ben what had happened to me when I made that loan to that good-for-nothing Gerard Taylor."

"You didn't want to go to the police," Mr. Gordon said, "so—"

"So I went to Ben, who is a dear friend, and Ben tracked him down for me, as I knew he would. And Donald, look at this." Miss Essie picked up a small leather portfolio. "Not only did we march Gerard to the bank to get the money to cover what he 'borrowed' from me, but he also gave me this case to carry it in."

"You mean you actually got your money back?" asked Mr. Gordon.

"Donald, you look almost as shocked as Gerard did when we confronted him yesterday," Miss Essie said, enjoying her triumph. "He told me this nonsense about how he had really intended to pay me back. That must be why he tried to disappear by moving ninety miles away, without leaving a forwarding address."

"Well, I'm certainly happy for you." Mrs. Gordon

hugged Miss Essie. "This is wonderful news."

Tasha and Sarah hugged her, too. Mr. Gordon shook Mr. Houston's hand. "Thank you so much for helping my mother."

"I'd do anything to help Essie," Mr. Houston said.

Tasha and Sarah glanced at each other. Was this the beginning of another romance for Miss Essie? Sarah wondered.

"But what about Mr. Taylor?" Allison asked.

"I believe in letting bygones be bygones," Miss Essie said. "It was enough satisfaction for me to see that old goat's face when we caught him."

"But I thought you wanted to marry him," said Allison.

"Shush, girl," said Miss Essie quickly.

Mr. Houston turned abruptly to Miss Essie. "You wanted to what?"

"Oh, don't pay any attention to her," Miss Essie said. "Mr. Taylor was just a good friend. You know how children are."

"Right," said Mr. Gordon with a little smile. "Always jumping to conclusions."

"Mr. Houston, would you like to stay for dinner?" Mrs. Gordon asked.

"No, thank you. I've got to catch a train down at the station so that I can get home before it's too dark," explained Mr. Houston.

"Why?" Allison asked.

"Mr. Houston doesn't see very well at night," said

Miss Essie. "Come on, Ben, I'll drive you home. It's the least I can do."

After everyone said good-bye, Sarah and Tasha rushed upstairs to Sarah's room.

"So what do you think?" asked Tasha.

"I think it's great Miss Essie got her money back. And—"

"And it looks to me like Miss Essie got around in her younger days," said Tasha.

"I wonder how many more of her old boyfriends are going to show up," said Sarah.

Tasha laughed. "Maybe when you're in your seventies, Billy, Roy, Dave, José, and who knows who else will be knocking on your door."

Sarah playfully pushed her cousin to the door. "Oh, girl, get out of here."

PINE

Fifteen

"Sarah!" Kwame hissed across the hall from the guidance counselor's office. When Sarah walked over to the door, he whispered, "I want you to be the first to know. Sky just had a talk with Mr. Miller. He's transferring out of Murphy."

"Sky is leaving? When?" asked Sarah.

"Keep it down. I don't want the whole school to know," said Kwame.

Sarah laughed. "Hey, Kwame, the whole school already knows about how you talk. Anyone who goes to see Mr. Miller knows their business will be in the street within half an hour. Ever since you became his filing aide, the world has known his business. So tell me more, Mr. Brown. What's this about Sky?"

131

"Sky was admitted to another school, and Mr. Miller agreed that his records would be transferred next week," whispered Kwame.

"Yes, and . . ."

"I'll tell you more at 18 Pine St. I wouldn't want Mr. Miller to hear me talking to you. He might think that he can't talk around me. I don't want to blow my cover," said Kwame.

By the time Sarah got to 18 Pine St. later that day, Tasha, Kwame, April, and Dave were already at their regular table. Dave was leaning back in his seat, his arms folded over his chest. April, Kwame, and Tasha were huddled on the other side of the table. Sarah sat between Kwame and Dave. They all looked at Sarah.

"So, can I guess why everyone's so quiet?" asked Sarah.

"Sure," said Kwame. "You know half of it."

"Yeah. What you told me in the hallway. I guess everyone else here knows that Sky is transferring."

"That's only part of the bad news," Tasha said. She looked at Dave.

"Sky said he's going to the new school because they cut him a deal," Dave said. "He's going to be exempt from most academic classes. All he has to do is wood shop and some remedial math. He hasn't learned a thing."

"I wonder how Jennifer's doing." Tasha pushed a slice of pizza toward her cousin.

"I haven't seen her at all," said April.

"The girl must be having a fit," said Tasha.

"She's having a fit caused by that misfit she was going out with," Kwame said. He got up to get some pizza.

"Let's talk," said Dave quietly as he leaned over toward Sarah.

Sarah's heart raced. She'd been dreading this moment.

Sixteen

"Let's go outside—it's a nice day, and it'll be private," Dave said.

As they got up to put on their jackets, Sarah looked over to Tasha. Tasha smiled and gave her a thumbs-up. "One step at a time," Tasha had told her. Well, Sarah thought, this might be a big step.

"I just heard that you and José have been dating," said Dave once they got outside.

"So?" Sarah said defensively.

"So we're not married—I mean we're not even really going out—but I thought you'd tell me. Do you really like him?"

"Dave—" Sarah was suddenly holding back tears. Then she thought of Miss Essie, and of her independence, and she stood up straight and held Dave's arm and looked him in the eye. "Dave, you're wonderful. I love being with you, I love being your friend. When you're close to me, it feels wonderful. But I wonder if we're ready for a relationship, you and me. We need to figure out where we are, and we need to stop hurting each other."

Dave looked at her, and Sarah thought he was going to cry.

"Look, Dave, I don't know how I feel about José," she managed to say. "I know that it feels good to be with him, but I've also been holding back. I guess I'm not as comfortable with him as I am with you. I need your friendship, Dave." She paused.

"Sarah," Dave said as he took her hand. "Let's quit fooling around. You make me feel terrific, and I'd like to spend more time with you. I want to go out with you. If you don't want to go out with me, tell me now and stop dragging this out."

All at once, Sarah realized why she'd been hesitating with José. Falling in love wasn't like a math problem, where you added up all the good points and subtracted the bad ones. Her problems with José—the way he was so formal sometimes, and the trouble she'd had dealing with his Hispanic family—weren't the reason that she'd been holding back. The real reason was that she'd been waiting for Dave. Dave Hunter was the one for her. Her feelings when she was with Dave were so natural—they were so right.

Sarah turned to him and said, "How about a date on Friday night?"

"Deal."

Sarah leaned against the twisted oak tree that stood along the road leading to Murphy High. She'd promised to meet José there after school. The wind was picking up and dry leaves were brushing against her legs. She was nervous about seeing José, but it was time to level with him.

"Hello." José's voice startled Sarah.

"Hi," she said.

"I've been thinking about our meeting all afternoon," José said. "Of meeting you, and finding out if what I thought was true."

"What was that?" Sarah asked.

"That when I kissed you I could actually feel the sweetness of you," he said.

"José!" Sarah looked away.

"Look, I brought something for you." He pulled a piece of tissue paper from his pocket and handed it to her.

Sarah opened the tissue. Inside was a small medallion.

"My grandmother wore this at her wedding," José said, taking Sarah's hand.

"José, I can't take this," Sarah said. "It means too much to you."

"Like you," José said. "Sometimes I think you

mean too much to me. But I want you to have it, Sarah. It speaks for me. It says 'Sarah, I love you very much.' "

Sarah swallowed hard. She shook her head and handed the medallion back. "I can't take it," she said. She pulled her hand away. Touching him would make it too hard to tell him. "I do like you," she said. "But I can't take the medallion."

"You don't like it?" asked José.

"It's beautiful. That's not the problem." She tried not to notice the hurt expression on his face. "It's hard for me to explain."

"Take your time," he said. "What do you need to explain? I don't understand."

Sara sighed. "Do you remember the first time we met at 18 Pine St. and talked about being friends?" she said.

José nodded.

"Well, I meant what I said then about just being friends. But after that—you've been so terrific, and we had fun. I sort of lost myself and got confused. It's been so much fun being with you. You're so cute—I just didn't know what I wanted anymore."

José looked at her with his huge dark eyes. Sarah thought he looked like a lost puppy. She knew that he had figured out what she was going to say, but she needed to say it anyway. "José," she said gently as she took his hands in hers. "Now I do know what I want. I need to give my relationship with Dave another chance. This medallion belongs to someone else. I'm sorry. I—"

"Sarah," José whispered. "Don't say anything else. It's been great. I'll catch you later at 18 Pine." And then he turned and walked away.

As Sarah watched him leave, sadness washed over her. But what followed was relief. She felt she had done the right thing. She had gone with her heart, and it felt good.

PINE

Seventeen

"Jennifer, did he say he'd be here?" asked Sarah.

Jennifer shrugged. "You know Sky," she answered. "It's hard to pin him down."

"That means if he feels like it, he'll show," said Cindy. Sarah noticed that Cindy's braids had gotten much longer since last week. She wondered if Cindy had gotten the hair weave that they had discussed months ago. Sarah realized that with all the excitement over José, she hadn't talked to Cindy as much as she usually did.

Kwame took out a scrap of paper. "I don't have time for this foolishness. I have to make a phone call."

"Well, would you look at Mr. Important," Tasha said as Kwame walked away from the table.

Suddenly Kwame said, "Yo, man, how's it going?" Sky was walking over toward the table. He had on an open black leather baseball jacket, a black knit shirt, and black slacks. His gold chains gleamed. Sarah couldn't help thinking that he looked like a celebrity athlete.

"Get this. A party just for me." Sky sat down in Kwame's seat, ignoring the empty chair next to Jennifer.

"So, are you ready to make the move?" asked Dave.

"Sure enough, man. I called my man Strickland over at my new school the other day. We're already coming up with a dynamite strategy on the court."

Dave pushed his chair back from the table.

"I'm going to get our order," said Steve. He went to the counter.

Kwame returned from his phone call. "Hey, man, you're in my seat. But that's okay. Just let me get my books. I've got to leave. Something important has come up. See you around, Sky."

"Now there goes one strange dude," Sky said after Kwame left. "He's always got his nose in some book."

Jennifer excused herself and left the table. Sky turned to Dave. "Strickland told me they have some real fine women at the school," he said. "Are you sure you don't want to transfer with me?"

"I like Murphy just fine," Dave replied, winking at Sarah.

"And, in case you didn't notice, so do we women," said Tasha.

"And you are some of the finest women at Murphy. So is Jennifer," said Sky.

"You can hold the compliments," said Tasha as Jennifer returned.

"Sky, we thought we'd give you a sort of going-away present. Mr. Harris made us four of his special with-everything pizzas."

Steve and José returned with huge trays of food. When everyone's plate was filled up, Jennifer asked Sky, "Do you think you'll get a better shot at your SATs in your new school?"

Sky started laughing. He was laughing so hard that he had trouble speaking, "You just don't get it," he said. "You keep wasting your time worrying about me. You guys have one way to go, and that's the only thing you know. I'm flexible, man. I bend with the wind, and ride the tide."

Cindy had heard enough. She grabbed a slice of pizza and stood. "I have to go," she said. "I have a test tomorrow and I want to study."

"Yeah, me too," said Steve.

"Nice party," said April. She picked up her pink polka-dot purse and her books and left.

Dave, who had been quietly watching, turned to Sky. "Sky, I like basketball. I love to play to win. But I've never been able to figure out guys like you. You're the one who doesn't get it. I am one of those 'chumps' who studies a lot. And I have colleges interested in me already. Who's knocking at your door? You say you want to play for the NBA. Well, you can't even play a whole season at one high school. Check it out, man."

"The same long story?" Sky asked. "I thought you'd understand what I'm about, man. You don't have to be like me, but quit hassling me, okay?"

"Yeah, I hear you," Dave said. "Don't forget us, man."

"Hey, see you on the court," Sky said, smiling. He stood up. "Thank you for the 'party.' But I have to get going. See you around, Jennifer." He walked away from the table.

Sarah looked at Tasha. "Well, we tried," she said. "It's his choice, his life."

"We have all this food here," Dave said, sounding a little sad. "So where's the party?"

"Maybe it's here," Tasha said. "Maybe it's here if we don't walk away from it."

"Hey, here comes Kwame." Dave nodded toward the door.

Kwame came in and ambled over to the table. He grinned. "I was standing on the corner talking when Sky went past. I decided to come back and get his slice." The others laughed.

"Is everybody coming back?" Sarah asked.

"I sort of told them I would scout around and see if there was any food left," Kwame admitted. "Since there's more than enough for me, I'll tell them to come in," he said with a grin.

"So now you've become a pizza scout," Sarah said. "Is that what your life has turned out to be about, Kwame Brown?"

"I've decided that life is about two things, pizza and love. Right now I'm into my pizza stage."

"Oh, I'm so disappointed." Tasha frowned. "Just when I was in the mood—"

"Wait! Wait! My mood is changing," Kwame called out. "I think I'm going into my love stage."

"And just when I was in the mood for extra mushrooms and pepperoni!" Tasha said with a wide grin.

PINE

Eighteen

Tasha let out a low whistle. Sarah was wearing embroidered ballet slippers, black spandex tights, and a blouse that Tasha had designed. "Dressed for studying on a Friday night, girl?" Tasha teased.

"You think Dave will like it?" Sarah asked, ignoring her.

"Like it? Good thing the basketball season is over. He might forget how to dribble. Where are you going?"

Sarah smiled. "We're going to the mall and then out for burgers. An old-fashioned date with no pressure."

"Sarah, do you realize that you are literally floating on that rug? I think Dave Hunter has got you mesmerized," Tasha said.

147

Just then the doorbell rang. Sarah flew down the stairs, breathed deeply, and opened the door for Dave.

"Hello, Sarah. Is Miss Essie in?" asked Mr. Houston.

Sarah was so surprised it wasn't Dave, she burst out laughing. At that moment she realized how much she was looking forward to tonight's date.

"What's all that laughing?" Miss Essie called from the kitchen.

"Sorry, Miss Essie," Sarah responded as she caught her breath. "It's Mr. Houston here for you."

Miss Essie came out of the kitchen, followed by Sarah's parents. Miss Essie was wearing her peach chiffon gown, with a matching hat. Sarah thought she looked wonderful.

"Now you and Mr. Houston have a great time," said Mr. Gordon. "And don't worry about coming back too late." As he was talking, Dave walked through the open door. The sight of the entire family made him step back.

"We won't, son. And you have a nice night, too, Sarah," said Miss Essie as she left.

"Come on in, Dave," said Mrs. Gordon. "It's good to see you."

Dave was wearing sneakers, jeans, and a new Nike sweatshirt. When he saw Sarah, his jaw dropped. "I thought we were just going for burgers."

"So, is there a law against looking nice at the

burger place?" Sarah answered.

"Absolutely not, Sarah. Not when you look that good." Dave smiled.

"Be back before midnight, okay?" said Mrs. Gordon.

"No problem." Dave smiled again. Sarah thought he had been smiling a lot since they'd agreed to go out. This would definitely be a night to remember, she thought.

As the two of them walked down the driveway to Dave's car, she heard her little sister's voice at the front door, and she turned toward the house.

"When do I start dating, Dad?" asked Allison.

Mr. Gordon grabbed his youngest daughter and hugged her. "Too soon, my little one, too soon."

Coming in Book 6, Fashion By Tasha

Fighting back tears of rage and frustration, Tasha marched over to Orchid. She turned away as the thin girl, still dressed in a gold two-piece outfit with a bare midriff, flipped through the sketches.

"Mmmm . . . nice . . . oh . . . oh, dear—"

Tasha had had enough. "Give me that!" she demanded, grabbing her portfolio.

"You have one or two good pieces," Orchid said. "I liked the shoulder lines in particular, but the rest of it is a little . . . ordinary. Don't you think so?"

Tasha gave her an icy stare.

When Tasha gets offered a job designing a line of clothing for a major European clothing manufacturer, it seems like the chance of a lifetime.

But then Tasha decides that the only way she can make her deadline is to drop out of school.

Is Tasha about to launch an exciting new career . . . or make the biggest mistake of her life?